Desire flared in Roarke....

For a week he'd been wondering what it would be like to kiss C.J. To taste her. Now, only inches away, her lips were parted, moist. It was time to find out. Slowly he leaned forward.

Wide-eyed, C.J. braced herself against the desk. But her defenses began to crumble the moment she felt the heat of his breath on her lips. For a second, his mouth was warm and full on hers. Then she felt his lips brush the corner of her mouth and feather kisses along her jaw. They left a trail of fire and ice. Why wasn't she pushing Roarke away? When his teeth scraped her bottom lip, she lost all control. There was pleasure, sharp and sweet as his tongue moved over hers. Her hands moved to frame his face, and grasp his silky hair. "You're out of order, Counselor," she murmured.

He was out of order? Roarke drew in a shaky breath. What was C.J. doing to him? He'd felt desire before. Wild and reckless. Warm and needy. But no woman had ever made him feel like *this*. He wanted nothing more than to crush her to him...and feel nothing more between them than hot, naked flesh....

Carolyn Andrews wrote *C.J.'s Defense* after serving on a jury several years ago. She found the legal process fascinating and decided two opposing lawyers would make great romance characters—and we agree! *C.J.'s Defense* was also a finalist in the 1993 Romance Writers of America contest for new writers. Carolyn and her husband and their three sons live in Syracuse, New York.

C.J.'s DEFENSE
CAROLYN ANDREWS

Harlequin Books

TORONTO • NEW YORK • LONDON
AMSTERDAM • PARIS • SYDNEY • HAMBURG
STOCKHOLM • ATHENS • TOKYO • MILAN
MADRID • WARSAW • BUDAPEST • AUCKLAND

To Janet Frances Fulgenzi, my mom and my best friend.
Special thanks to James P. Murphy for his legal expertise,
and to my sister writers, Maria, Peg and Garda
for their support.

ISBN 0-373-25598-5

C.J.'S DEFENSE

This edition published by arrangement with Harlequin Enterprises B. V.

® and TM are trademarks of the publisher. Trademarks indicated with
® are registered in the United States Patent and Trademark Office, the
Canadian Trade Marks Office and in other countries.

Printed in U.S.A.

1

IT WAS A LONELY PLACE to run. Scary even. C. J. Parker suppressed a shiver as she climbed over a guardrail and jogged down a steep incline to the deserted track. Why had she allowed Mrs. Williams to talk her into this? The air, still damp from an all-night rain, carried the scent of decay. An odor well suited to her surroundings, she thought, as she gazed down at the roof of Monroe High School.

The school had been built at the foot of one of Syracuse's many hills, its track and football field carved neatly out of the hillside above. Once it might have been lovely, surrounded by grass and trees. Now weeds competed for space with litter, and run-down buildings pressed in on all sides.

C.J. pushed through a rusted gate and began to run around the gravel track, past sagging bleachers and an announcer's booth covered with peeling graffiti. It was certainly not the setting one would imagine for a state track star. But according to his mother, Tony Williams ran here every morning at six o'clock.

On the road above, a city bus groaned as it began the long climb to the college at the top of the hill. She glanced up to follow its slow progress, and for a few moments she felt less alone and vulnerable. Then a movement behind the bus caught her attention. A lone runner had turned onto the street. Tony? No, there was nothing boyish about the runner's muscular build. Her heart skipped a beat. No need to panic, she told herself as he moved closer. Still, the instant the man spotted her, her skin prickled with fear and her fingers closed around the travel-size can of hair spray in her pocket. It wasn't mace, but in a pinch... She didn't take her hand out of her pocket until the man moved through the intersection and on up the hill.

So intent was she on the stranger that she wasn't aware of a second runner on the track until she heard the crunch and scatter of gravel directly behind her. This time her heart flipped all the way up to her throat and didn't settle until he ran past and she saw the Monroe High sweatshirt. She chased him for half a lap before she could speak. "Tony Williams?"

When he didn't reply, C.J. increased her pace, slanting him a quick glance as she drew even with him. The mug shot in his file was a good likeness. "You *are* Tony Williams?"

"If you're a reporter—"

"No. I'm an attorney. C. J. Parker."

"I already have a lawyer." He lengthened his stride.

Gritting her teeth, C.J. did the same. Mrs. Williams had warned her that it wouldn't be easy. Tony had given up, she'd said. And with the trial only a week away, his court-appointed defense counsel wanted to plead the boy guilty and try for a deal with the District Attorney.

C.J. drew in a deep breath. At this speed she would have to make every word count. "Your mom came to see me yesterday. She asked me to take over your case. Mr. Fallon has no objection."

When the boy didn't reply, C.J. allowed the silence between them to lengthen, hoping that he would be tempted to break it. If he talked, she might not have to. One lap became two. She tried to ignore the fact that her lungs were on fire.

For as long as she could remember she'd wanted to be her father's partner. And she'd known that it wouldn't be easy. But she had never once pictured herself literally running after clients. Ridiculous. Her lips curved briefly in a smile.

By the end of a mile, the humor of the situation had worn thin. C.J. could feel the push of wind each time they rounded the curve at the far end of the track. Tony seemed oblivious to it. His breathing was silent, effortless. She was beginning to huff and puff.

"How many of . . . these do you do?" she managed to ask.

"Ten."

"Laps?"

"Miles."

C.J.'s heart plummeted. She dragged in a breath and said, "Come to my office. After school. We'll talk."

Tony pulled past her. Head down, C.J. struggled to close the gap. Longer legs, that's what she needed. Just as she drew even with him, he leapt onto the grass verge and headed for the gate that led down to the school. With a final burst of speed, she surged past him and collapsed against it.

"I'm finishing on the streets. You want to come along?"

C.J. stared at him, trying to figure out if he was a sadist or merely a comedian. "I'll pass," she panted finally, fishing a business card out of her pocket. "My office. Three o'clock." Two-word sentences were her limit.

"About what?"

"Your case," she replied.

The boy's laugh had a bitter ring to it. "Right. I told everything I know to Mr. Fallon. Now he wants me to plead guilty. What are you going to do? Save me?"

Good question, C.J. thought, and a challenging one to answer in two words. "I'll try."

He pulled on the gate. She pushed. For a moment their eyes met and held. "Why are you doing this?" he asked.

For the first time C.J. saw frustration and anger on his face, and she thought of the woman who had come to her office the day before. "Your mother."

The flicker of pain in his eyes was brief, gone in a flash. C.J. held her card out to him again. This time he took it and stuffed it into his pocket. The moment she stepped out of his path, he pulled the gate open and ran down the hill. Shaking her head, she watched until he disappeared around the school building. What had she gotten herself into? The boy's case held as much promise as his surroundings. Still, he hadn't given up entirely. He was still running ten miles a day training for the state track finals.

THE MOMENT HE CRESTED the hill at the top of College Avenue, Roarke Farrell turned to get another look at the Monroe High track half a mile below him.

Why would any sane woman run laps around a deserted football field at six in the morning? That was the question that had nagged him all the way up the hill. He'd charted a course that had allowed him to catch occasional glimpses of her. Now, jogging in place, he waited until he spotted her white sweatshirt. Why was she wearing white? Anyone who was out at this hour could see her. He swore and began his descent into the city.

Where were her brains? Concern for her warred with annoyance. Why didn't she join a health club?

For two blocks buildings obstructed Roarke's view of the track. Muttering an oath, he ran faster. She wasn't any of his business. That's what he'd told himself when he'd first spotted her. But if she ended up the victim of a violent crime, her case would eventually cross his desk. Over the years, he'd learned to value prevention over prosecution.

Roarke made a quick right into a parking lot, and for a few seconds he once again had a clear view of the track. No sign of her. He didn't panic. Bleachers blocked half the field from this angle. He vaulted a guardrail and cut through a short alley. At the end, he once more saw the flash of white. The knot in his stomach loosened, then tightened again as a bus discharged three passengers a block away from her. To his relief they headed in his direction.

He lost sight of her again as he sprinted through the final intersection. Women! In his thirty-six years, he'd learned a lot about them. His mother and two sisters had seen to that. But he didn't understand them. This one was about to receive some friendly advice.

It was only as he raced down the steep incline to the track that he noticed she wasn't alone. A tall youth in gray sweats stood inside the gate that led down to the school. Friend or foe, he wondered as he watched her hand the kid something. A transaction? Circumstances favored an illegal one. With a sigh, Roarke began to walk across the field. When he was halfway to the gate, the kid took off.

C.J. saw him the moment she turned around. Panic bubbled up instantly, and then she recognized him. The lone runner. Her heartbeat steadied. Hills were hell. Obviously he had given up and decided to use the track. A wise decision unless you were trying to keep up with the state cross-country champion. Taking a deep breath, she began to walk back along the upper curve.

Her relief evaporated the instant she saw him adjust his course to intercept her. Her mind raced as she gauged the distance to the opposite gate. She wouldn't be able to outrun him. Not after racing with Tony and not up that hill to her car. When he stepped onto the gravel, she stopped and took his measure. He was taller than average, not quite six feet. Up close, she was even more aware of his solid build. His legs were lean and muscled, his shoulders wide, and his face set along stern lines. She felt her muscles tighten and willed them to relax. She'd handled much larger men in her self-defense class. Her fingers closed around the small can in her pocket. If only she could see his eyes. But she didn't want him to get that close. She pulled the hair spray out and waved it at him. "I've got mace."

Roarke pulled up short. "Hold it. I didn't mean to scare you. I thought that young man might be giving you trouble."

C.J. didn't lower the can. "I'm fine. He's my client."

"Client?" Roarke's eyes narrowed as he made a thorough inspection from the reddish gold hair that was pulled back into a ponytail to the scuffed running shoes.

The baggy white sweats successfully camouflaged her figure. "Just what kind of services do you provide?"

Her chin lifted at his mocking tone. "Certainly not the kind you're implying."

"This is a hell of a place to conduct business of any kind."

She waved the can at him. "I can take care of myself."

He'd been about to back away, but her words stopped him. Did she really believe that mace made her invincible? Moving quickly, he clipped her wrist with the edge of his hand and sent the can sailing in a wide arc to the ground. He whirled her around and pulled her against him, trapping her arms at her side.

C.J. went perfectly still.

"It's all right," he said. "I'm not going to hurt you. I just wanted to demonstrate how ineffective mace can be." When she showed no sign of putting up a struggle, he released his hold and stepped back.

The elbow she rammed into his stomach forced his breath out in a whoosh. Already off-balance, he had no chance to deflect the blow to his neck that sent him slamming into the ground.

For a few moments he lay perfectly still, struggling for a breath. Stones pressed into his skin. Dampness seeped through his clothes. He drew in a second breath and used it to swear.

"Are you all right?"

Stunned, he turned his head and stared at her. She was right there on the other side of the fence. At least she'd had the good sense to get behind it. She'd have a head start if he could summon up the strength to climb over it and attempt to strangle her. Roarke levered himself up on one elbow and groaned. Maybe climbing the fence wasn't such a good idea.

"My car is at the top of the hill," she said. "I'll stop at the first phone and call an ambulance. Just lie still until they get here."

Roarke answered by rolling to his feet in one relatively smooth movement. He managed to keep from wincing until she jumped back from the fence and turned to race up the hill.

It gave him some satisfaction to see her stumble and fall twice before she reached her car, a white Volkswagen Bug. By the time she stalled it in the middle of the intersection, he was smiling. What kind of a woman knocked a man flat and then came back to see if he was all right?

Shaking his head, he leaned over to brush gravel off the back of his legs. It was then that he spotted the mace. When he picked it up and discovered it was hair spray, he stared in the direction her car had taken. Nerve. She had more than her fair share of it. And whoever she was, she needed a keeper.

"I DON'T LIKE IT." Paul O'Shaughnessy paced back and forth in the small office. C.J. sat at her desk, hands folded, and waited for the storm to subside. In the six months since she'd moved to Syracuse to become her father's associate, he'd made one thing very clear: He did not want her to do defense work. The moment that Tony Williams had left, he'd barged into her office.

At the window, Paul turned to glare at her. "The Williams case is too dangerous."

C.J. said nothing. She was twenty-eight years old and had long ago learned that with Paul O'Shaughnessy silence was her best strategy. Arguing with the best defense attorney in upstate New York was a difficult and often futile experience. Her mother had never learned how to do it and win. But C.J. planned to succeed where her mother had failed.

"Your grandfather called the other day." Paul shoved his hands into his pockets and resumed his pacing. "He says your mother's office is all ready for you. Now that I'm fully recovered from my heart surgery, you ought to think of taking him up on his offer."

Pressing her lips firmly together, C.J. listened once again to her father argue the advantages of working for her grandfather. She knew the speech by heart. Eventually she would become a partner in one of the most prestigious law firms in Chicago. Why she might even get appointed to the bench, the way her mother had. What he neglected to mention was that in the meantime she'd have to work on enough estates and trusts to put her into a deep coma.

Still, she had to admit that her father made the case much more effectively than her grandfather did. At five foot eight with a slender, wiry build, Paul O'Shaughnessy gave the impression of being a much larger man. He had a presence, a kind of energy that grabbed the listener's attention. It made her think suddenly of the man at the track that morning.

She pushed the thought aside. Handling her father required all of her attention and skill. She met his eyes steadily when he stopped in front of her desk.

"Your grandfather has influence and power. How can you pass up an opportunity like this?"

It was a question C.J. couldn't answer. The fact was that in spite of everything her grandfather had done for her mother, she had died an unhappy woman. How could she say that to the one man who'd loved her mother as much as she had? Instead she smiled and said, "I'm here to stay. And I intend to defend Tony Williams."

"I don't like it," Paul muttered, pulling his hands out of his pockets to run them through his short, gray hair. "If you're determined to take on a criminal case, you might at least wait for one you have a chance of winning."

C.J. raised her eyebrows. "Of course. That's the way you built your reputation, isn't it? You only took the easy ones."

He glared at her. "Never mind how I built my reputation."

She smiled knowingly at him. "Do as I say, not as I do. Is that it? Besides, haven't you always warned me that no case is a sure thing?"

"Hmph." He began to pace again. "This one looks like a sure enough win for the prosecution. That young college student may suffer permanent brain damage. What does Williams have to say for himself?"

"He can't remember hitting Danny Jasper with the baseball bat. He doesn't even remember getting it out of his car."

"Temporary amnesia?" Paul looked skeptical. "You think he's telling the truth?"

"He was examined by a doctor who claims it's a possibility. And it would explain his apathy. He's afraid he may have done it."

Scowling, Paul sat on the corner of her desk. "It'll be tough to sell that to a jury. You talked to Bill Fallon?"

"At length. He was only too happy to send over Tony's complete file."

"He's probably been praying for someone to take it off his hands. Any idea of his trial strategy?"

"Self-defense."

Paul's crack of laughter filled the room. "A baseball bat against bare fists? I'd love to see him try to make a jury buy that."

"You have a better idea?"

He shrugged. "Pull a Perry Mason and lay the blame on somebody else."

C.J. frowned. "Five witnesses swear that they saw Tony standing over Danny with the bat in his hands."

Paul stood up, his displeasure obvious. "Why did you take this case?"

C.J. went to him and put her arms around him. "Because I want to do defense work. Because I've been here for over six months and the only time I've been inside a courtroom is to watch you. And even though I can learn a lot from watching an expert, sooner or later, I have to try a case myself. Besides, what if Tony is innocent?"

"What if he's guilty as hell and decides to take a swing at you with his bat?"

C.J. drew back, dropping her hands to her sides. "When are you going to realize that I can take care of myself?"

"When are you going to realize that practicing criminal law is too dangerous and take your grandfather up on his offer? He can open doors for you."

"I can open my own doors."

A knock at the door prevented Paul's reply. Ruth Singer breezed into the room. "Am I interrupting?"

C.J. managed a smile for the older woman who was much more than a secretary to them both. "You're just in time to save me from another lecture on the perils of practicing criminal law."

Ruth took Paul's arm and urged him toward the connecting door to his office. "In that case, I'll tell Sandra Hughes you're free. She says it's urgent. I can finish the lecture for you. I know it by heart."

"Very funny." At the door he turned back to C.J. "If the Williams boy is innocent, who's the next best candidate?"

"Two of his classmates identified him as the one holding the bat. It's odd that they would finger their own friend."

"Do either of them have any previous arrests?"

"No."

Paul walked back to her desk. "Give me their names."

C.J. hesitated for a moment and then wrote the names on a slip of paper. Paul tucked it into his wallet. "Sam Hillerman is doing some work for me on the Hughes case. He might be able to turn up something in their juvenile records."

"Aren't they supposed to be sealed?"

"Sometimes the glue doesn't stick so well."

Ruth cleared her throat.

"Okay. Okay." Paul began to back away. "You'll need to get a postponement. Which judge shall I call?"

"None of them," C.J. replied. Then she smiled and softened her tone. "You have your hands full with the Hughes trial."

"And she happens to be waiting to see you right now." Ruth shooed Paul out and closed the door behind him.

"I know exactly what you're going to say," C.J. said. Ruth had been Paul's secretary for as long as she could remember. She had always run his office with a rather terrifying efficiency that left him free to devote his energies to the practice of law. Over the years only her hair color had changed. It was lighter, grayer, and the only indication that she might be the grandmother of three.

"I was only going to congratulate you," Ruth said mildly. "He was so upset when he stormed in on you, and now he's thinking of ways to help you out. You know just how to handle him."

C.J. paced back and forth in front of her desk, unconsciously retracing Paul's earlier path. "And now you're handling me."

"He can't help worrying about you. He's your father."

C.J. threw up her hands. "He goes way beyond worrying. In six months he hasn't given me anything more dangerous to do than get a few speeding tickets dismissed. He refuses to let me help with the Hughes trial because she's accused of murder. And if he can't find a way to scare me off Tony's case, he'll try to take it over. He's impossible!"

"He certainly is."

"And stubborn."

"Definitely."

"And chauvinistic."

"I don't know how I've managed to put up with him for the last twenty-five years."

C.J. tried to glare, but the twinkle in Ruth's eyes was having the desired effect. "He'd much rather I would leave and go back to work for Grandad in Chicago."

"Well, if he's singing that song again, he must really be feeling better."

C.J. had to smile. "I guess that's one way of looking at it."

"Besides, even though half the time he's trying to persuade you to go back to Chicago, the other half he's doodling 'O'Shaughnessy and O'Shaughnessy' in the margins of his legal pads."

"Really?"

Ruth raised her right hand. "I swear. Don't you know that there's a part of your father that wants the whole world to know that his daughter has joined his firm?"

"I'm not going to change my mind about that. No one is going to know that he's my father until I have a chance to build a reputation on my own. Until then, he's Paul O'Shaughnessy, and I'm C. J. Parker, the lucky attorney he's taken on as his associate." She began to pace again. "And I'm not going to be his partner until I earn it." At the window she turned and shoved her hands into the pockets of her jacket. "He'd better change his doodles, too. I'm going to stick with my mother's maiden name. That's the way the letterhead read before she left."

Ruth smiled. "You're just like your father."

C.J. shot her an amused look. "If that's your polite way of telling me that I'm impossible and stubborn, I'll plead guilty. But I'm no chauvinist."

Ruth laughed. "Agreed."

"You probably think I'm a fool to turn down any help I can get on Tony's case."

Ruth shrugged innocently. "I wouldn't have phrased it quite that way. But it does seem to me that one of the perks of working in the same office as your father is to be able to tap into his expertise. And you seem to be doing that."

C.J. let out a long breath. "You're right, of course. Should I ask him to give Judge Kaufmann a call?"

"Only if you fail at the District Attorney's office. I just finished speaking to Kevin Wilson's secretary. He's the one you have to talk to about the Williams case, and she says he'll be tied up in court until five."

"Thanks." She hugged Ruth on her way out the door.

C.J. opened her umbrella and hurried down the steps of her office building. The rain had been falling steadily all afternoon, but it was not the weather that quickened her steps. Usually she enjoyed the five-minute walk to the courthouse, but today she didn't want to be alone with her thoughts. All day long that man at the track had been slipping into them whenever he got the chance.

At the corner she waited for the light, her foot tapping on the curb. Even now she could remember every emotion that had ripped through her during the mad race to her car. Panic when she'd tripped and hit the ground, terror that he might be right behind her. He'd scared her half to death, and she shouldn't have wasted even a minute of her time worrying about him.

But she couldn't get him out of her mind, especially his voice. The light changed, and C.J. ran across the street. She'd heard his voice before. Not in person. He was not a man she could have forgotten. She recalled the way her skin had prickled when he'd first looked at her from the road above the track. If she closed her eyes, she could see the lean, muscled length of his legs. She could feel the hard strength of those arms. Swearing, she hopped out of the puddle she'd just waded into.

The voice, Parker. Keep your mind on the voice. It was very deep. And . . . controlled. Had she heard it on the radio? Nothing in his tone or diction eliminated the possibility. But maybe she'd heard it on the phone. That would be more likely. Perhaps he was one of her father's clients, one of his low-life, criminal clients. No. She rejected the idea as she stepped off the curb to detour around a delivery truck blocking the sidewalk. There had been an air of authority about the man. If he was a criminal, he would be a leader. A crime boss who needed Paul O'Shaughnessy's skill to keep out of jail?

Overhead, thunder cracked, and a gust of wind sent a spray of water against her legs. A bad omen, C.J. thought as she pulled her umbrella closer. Somehow she was sure that the truth would be much worse than anything she could imagine.

The moment she spotted Kevin Wilson hurrying down the courthouse steps, her spirits lifted. At least the prosecutor handling Tony's case was someone she knew. She'd had to deal with him when she'd negotiated the traffic violations for her father's clients. It was not the kind of work she'd envisioned when she'd gone to law school, but it had allowed her to get to know some of the people in the District Attorney's office. And as her father was so fond of saying, knowledge was strength.

"Great timing, huh?" C.J. asked as she intercepted Kevin and lifted her umbrella to accommodate his greater height.

He scowled at her. "Who's been speeding this time?"

"It's nothing like that," she assured him. "I just need a minute." Matching two steps to his one, she managed to keep them both dry while they crossed the street and entered the City Office Building.

Once inside, Kevin shook his head. "It's not a good time. I'll be here half the night preparing for court tomorrow."

"A minute. I promise it's all I'll need."

Neither of them spoke on the ride to the fifteenth floor. C.J. used the time to plan her strategy.

She studied Kevin as he stared into space. Like other prosecutors she'd known when she'd worked in Chicago, he was ambitious and dedicated primarily to the advancement of his own career. When he'd cooperated with her in the past, he'd done so without any threat of negative consequences to himself. Agreeing to postpone Tony's trial would be different. The press, having already convicted the boy, would not be happy about the delay.

Following him down the hall and into his office, she decided on a direct approach. As soon as he had discarded his jacket and slumped into his chair, she said, "I want a postponement in the Tony Williams case."

Kevin's head snapped up. She saw the surprise in his eyes quickly replaced by amusement. He leaned back and clasped his hands behind his head. "So Bill Fallon finally unloaded it. I thought O'Shaughnessy was smarter than that."

C.J. decided not to correct his mistake. If he thought it was her father's case, it might work in her favor. "We're going to ask Judge Kaufmann for two months. Any objection?"

"Whoa!" Kevin leaned forward. "Time-out. You're going to have to discuss this with my boss."

C.J. frowned. "I thought you were handling the case."

"Under Roarke's supervision. He makes all the major decisions. And speak of the devil." Kevin's eyes moved past C.J. to the man who had just appeared in the doorway. "Roarke, you'll never guess. Fallon dumped the Williams case on Paul O'Shaughnessy."

As soon as C.J. heard the name, the memory she'd been searching for all day slipped into place. Roarke Farrell. Could the man she'd flattened at the track have been Roarke Farrell, the acting District Attorney? She didn't turn around. Perhaps she was mistaken. But she felt the skin on the back of her neck prickle the same way it had when he'd first looked at her.

"Kevin, I'm sorry I missed your cross-examination of Mumford. How did it go?" Roarke asked.

Fists clenched, stomach sinking, C.J. kept her eyes on Kevin Wilson as he described his day in court. No wonder the voice had seemed familiar. She'd taken enough of his messages for her father. Maybe he wouldn't recognize her. And maybe she could just vanish in a puff of smoke.

Roarke leaned against the door, listening with half his mind while he studied the woman standing in front of him. Even from the back she drew his attention. Slender, not very tall. Her suit was the color of ripe raspberries. His glance dropped to where it fit snugly across her hips, then returned to her hair. Something, perhaps the color, tugged at his memory. It was blond with hints of red, and she wore it pulled back into a neat braid. Loosened, it would fall below her shoulders. And in spite of the hint of fire, it would have the cool, light texture of silk. The moment he realized the direction his thoughts had taken, his eyes narrowed.

Recognition came the moment she turned around. And it was mutual. He could see it in her eyes. He waited, not speaking until Kevin at long last remembered to make the introductions. "This is C. J. Parker. She works in Paul O'Shaughnessy's office."

Roarke's brow creased in the barest hint of a frown. Why didn't he know that his old friend Paul had hired an associate? That's what came of becoming a paper pusher instead of a trial lawyer. Suppressing a surge of annoyance, he stepped forward and extended his hand. She grasped it without hesitation. Her palm was dry, but not soft. No, it wouldn't be. He could still remember the swift, sure blow she had delivered to the side of his neck. When she would have withdrawn her hand, he held on to it for a moment longer.

"C.J. is here to ask a favor," Kevin was saying.

"Indeed." Roarke smiled at her. "Why don't you step into my office? We'll discuss it."

2

IT WAS DEFINITELY NOT a friendly smile, C.J. decided as she followed him out of the room. Her gaze traveled slowly from the dark hair curling over the collar of his shirt to his narrow waist and hips. He had the solid, wedgelike build of a boxer. Even from the back, he radiated a raw strength and energy that had her muscles tensing. She willed them to relax. After all, he wasn't going to attack her. Not physically at least.

At the end of the hall, he turned and led the way down another corridor. She doubled her pace to keep up. At least their encounter at the track hadn't left him walking with a limp. Of course, she couldn't discount internal injuries. The male ego bruised very easily.

But then, Roarke Farrell was reputed to be tough. And ruthless. Both qualities were typical in the prosecutors she'd known. Still, in his six years as an assistant District Attorney, Roarke had won her father's admiration and respect. For several months he'd been absent from the courtroom, filling in for his ailing boss. That was why she hadn't yet seen him in action. Correction, she thought ruefully as she watched him turn into his office. She'd seen Roarke in action all right. Up close and personal. The memory tightened the knot in her stomach.

The phone rang as Roarke reached his desk. He lifted the receiver. "Farrell here."

C.J. lingered in the doorway, grateful for the reprieve. The room was literally overflowing with files.
They covered every surface and lined the walls, spilling their contents out in uneven lines toward the center
of the floor.

"Only about as busy as you are, I imagine." The affection in his tone brought C.J.'s attention back to him.
She blinked, then watched in fascination as the stern
lines of his face suddenly softened. Was this the same
man she'd flattened at the track? Oh, the strength was
still there. Her gaze moved from the high, wide cheek-
bones to the firm line of his chin. Dangerous was the
word she would have used to describe him this morning. But now when he was smiling . . .

It was only when he frowned at her and waved her
into the room that she realized she was staring. Quickly
she gathered her scattered thoughts and picked a careful path through the clutter.

"Slow down. Read it again." Roarke tucked the
phone under his chin and lifted files off the nearest
chair. C.J. noticed that he glanced through them before sorting them into different piles. Was this organized chaos?

He cleared another chair. "I can look it over but . . ."
He glanced at his watch. "Give me twenty minutes."

"Problem?" she asked as he hung up.

"Family. Won't you sit down, Ms. Parker?"

C.J. chose the nearest chair. When he sat next to her,
she recognized the ploy. He was trying to put her at
ease. Not that he had a chance. Still, she was surprised
at the effort it took to keep from shifting farther back
in her chair.

"So you work for Paul O'Shaughnessy."

"He's been kind enough to rent me office space and refer a few cases to me."

"I envy you. He's been my idol since I was fourteen. I used to sneak into the back of the courtroom to watch him in action. I even dreamed of working with him one day."

C.J.'s eyes widened. "Why didn't you then?"

Roarke shrugged. "By the time I graduated from law school, I had other responsibilities." He lifted a hand, then dropped it. "Different priorities. I still go to see him whenever he tries a case. He's the best trial lawyer in the state."

"Yes." C.J.'s smile was spontaneous and unguarded, and for a moment Roarke lost his train of thought. All he could see were her eyes. They were golden brown, the color of very old whiskey. And her skin. It was pale and flawless except for a sprinkle of freckles across her nose. And her mouth . . . With an effort, he collected himself. It was the second time she'd caught him off guard. A well aimed self-defense move he could understand. But a smile? "What exactly do you want, Ms. Parker?"

With an effort, she held herself still under his steady regard. No wonder she had remembered his voice. She could almost feel it brushing along her skin. The man could probably charm snakes with it. Her fingers tightened on the arms of the chair. And there was the matter of their earlier encounter. Was he going to ignore it? Suddenly she couldn't. "Before we go into what I want, I'd like to apologize for what happened this morning at the track."

It was the third time she'd surprised him, and this time he grinned. He'd learned long ago that sometimes in life it was better to go with the flow. "I was hoping we could forget about that." He rubbed the side of his neck. "I've been trying to all day. What were you doing there anyway?"

"I was running."

"No." He looked thoughtful. "I don't think so. That's a dangerous section of the city for a woman to run in alone. You must have had a good reason to take a risk like that."

C.J. said nothing even as the silence stretched between them. One of the first cross-examination techniques she'd picked up from her father was to give the witness time to fill in the blanks. She wasn't about to be tricked by it.

"You said the young man was a client," Roarke continued, then suddenly snapped his fingers. "Of course. Tony Williams runs track for Monroe High. I can't believe that Paul approved of your meeting him there."

Her chin shot up. "It's my case and it was my decision."

"I thought Kevin said Paul was handling it."

"Mr. Wilson assumed I was here on Mr. O'Shaughnessy's behalf."

"Ah, I see."

He did, too. C.J. found herself admiring his perception and cursing it at the same time. It was time to take the initiative. "What were *you* doing at the track, Mr. Farrell?"

"I was running."

C.J. shook her head. "I don't think so. You started up the hill to the college. Why did you come back and accost me?"

"Accost?" His eyebrows rose. "An interesting choice of words, Ms. Parker. You're the one who threatened me, as I recall. With mace."

"And you knocked it out of my hand. How was I supposed to know that you weren't some mad rapist?"

"That area has one of the highest crime rates in the city. How was I supposed to know that you weren't engaging in some illegal activity? Prostitution, drugs—"

"You actually thought that I . . ."

Roarke smiled. "I thought of several possibilities, but what I finally decided was that you were a brainless, newly transplanted yuppie who might benefit from some friendly advice."

"You thought . . ." She rose from the chair as her words turned into a sputter. "You decided . . ." She whirled, wanting to cool her anger before she gave in to the urge to punch him. Two steps brought her up against a stack of files. Frustrated, she turned and walked right into him.

Heart hammering, she took a quick step back and poked a finger into his chest. "Why you simpleminded, egotistical, overprotective . . ."

She was about to poke him again when he began to laugh. The sound, rich and bright, filled the room and immediately distracted her.

"What's so funny?" she demanded.

Her eyes, when they met his, were still dark with temper.

Lifting his hand, Roarke stepped back. "Look, I'm not anxious to end up flat on my back again. How about if I apologize?"

She opened her mouth and shut it. Her anger hadn't yet run its course, but she couldn't recall the last time she'd let it loose like this. With her hands clenched into fists, she counted to ten. Was it because of that sudden surge of heat she'd felt when she'd walked into him? No, she pushed the thought aside. It was because he was partially right. That was what had made her lose control for a minute. Going alone to the track to meet a client accused of assault had been risky. The fact that his mother believed in Tony's innocence had convinced her the risk was minimal. But she wasn't about to explain that to Roarke Farrell, and he shouldn't have interfered. She opened her mouth to tell him just that when she remembered what she'd come to see him for. She needed his help. She took a deep steadying breath and said, "All right. I accept your apology."

Roarke couldn't suppress a grin as he gestured her into her chair and sat in his own. He had lived with his own temper all of his life, and he could appreciate her struggle for control. "You know I can't help but admire how you did that."

"What?"

"Reined yourself in." He watched with some satisfaction as her eyes widened. Good. He didn't want to be the only one feeling surprised. Extending his hand, he said, "Why don't we wipe the slate clean and start all over again?"

Suddenly and completely charmed, C.J. moved forward in her chair to grasp his hand. Her leg brushed against his, and for just a moment she became intensely aware of him, the strength of his fingers, the warmth of his skin, the hardness of his thigh. And his eyes. This close they were more blue than gray. If she continued to look into them, she just might believe anything he said.

Roarke tightened his grip on her hand when she tried to withdraw it. For just a second his mind went completely blank. For just a second an image, very clear, of her lips, moist and curved in a smile, and an impression, very distinct, of softness and the promise of heat, pushed every other thought aside. It was enough to make desire twist, hot and tight, in the pit of his stomach. Roarke released her hand, rose and walked to stand behind his desk. Going with the flow was fine in some instances, but it could be very dangerous in uncharted waters.

The distance that Roarke put between them eased the funny, burning sensation in C.J.'s chest. Facing him across the desk, she suddenly found it easier to force her mind back to the business at hand. "I want a two-month postponement in the Williams trial."

"Judge Kaufmann is the man to ask," Roarke replied.

"He'd respond more favorably if I can tell him that you have no objection."

"I'm sure he would."

She tried a smile. "Look, it can't mean that much to you." She waved a hand at the stack of files. "You obviously have other cases that you could work on."

"True. And if it were any other trial, I'd help you out. But my boss is an elected official. The college carries a lot of weight in this city. Naturally they're concerned when a student is injured so close to the campus."

"So the public relations problems of the school take priority over the life of an innocent boy?"

Roarke opened a file and withdrew an X ray. He placed it on the desk between them and traced the outline of a nearly white area with one finger. "The doctor will testify that the damage to Danny Jasper's brain might be permanent."

Though she'd studied the X ray before, C.J. couldn't prevent her throat from tightening. Keeping her eyes steady on Roarke's, she said, "What happened to Danny Jasper is a tragedy. But rushing to convict my client won't change that."

"Rushing? This case has been on the docket for over a month. Hasn't it occurred to you that this last-minute change of lawyers is just a delaying tactic and that your client is merely using you to abuse the system?"

"That's not true." C.J. rose to her feet. "But even if it were, you and I both know that Tony has the right to use me and you and the entire legal system to get a fair trial. Or have you forgotten that he's innocent until he's proven guilty?"

"Fine words, Ms. Parker. But if I were you, I'd save them for a jury. You're going to need every one of them after they hear five witnesses testify that they saw Tony Williams standing over Danny Jasper's body with the bat in his hand."

C.J. placed her palms flat on the desk and leaned forward. "You can't produce anyone who actually saw him hit Danny."

Roarke inserted the X ray carefully into the file and closed it. "I'll still get my conviction. And I will not help you get a two-month postponement."

"A month then."

"Two weeks." The words were out before he could stop them. Annoyance warred briefly with admiration for his opponent before the latter won out. After all there was no harm done. Judge Kaufmann would give her at least that long.

C.J. gave him a brief nod. "I'll mention your offer to the judge when I ask for two months."

Roarke watched her turn and maneuver through the piles of manila folders. She was good. Paul was training her well.

C.J. sidestepped the last stack of files only to collide with a woman who suddenly rushed into the room.

"Whoops. Sorry." When she reached for C.J.'s arm to steady herself, the paper she was holding fluttered to the floor. C.J. stooped to pick it up.

"Thanks. You saved my life. This could have been lost forever in this mess." She winked at C.J. before turning her attention to Roarke. "How do you get any work done in here?"

C.J. smiled as she watched the older woman negotiate the maze of files to Roarke's desk. He took the document, then leaned over to kiss her cheek before beginning to read it. Curious, C.J. lingered in the doorway. With their heads so close, the resemblance was striking. They had the same dark hair, the same classic features. The woman was older, but youthful in appearance with that lovely type of olive skin that never seemed to wrinkle. C.J. guessed her to be forty-something, perhaps early fifties. Roarke's older sister?

"It's a work stoppage order. You can't continue with the renovation."

The woman threw up her hands and turned to C.J. "Do I need a lawyer to tell me that? I can read." She turned back to Roarke. "Can't you do something? Get it revoked?"

Roarke looked at the paper again. "It's not that easy. The Shelby Mansion is a national landmark. That brings it under the jurisdiction of the Landmark Preservation Board, and they object to your plans to build a greenhouse on the back of the building. According to their research, there was no greenhouse on the grounds in 1870. It's well within their power to shut down the whole project."

"I can't believe it!" She turned to C.J. again. "Can you? I suppose that in 1870 there was a bank across the street that looked like a tacky Swiss chalet? Or a twenty-story building across the park?"

Roarke sighed. "You could always give up the idea of a greenhouse and put your restaurant on the first floor."

"No!" She slapped her hand down on a stack of files. "For seventeen years I have operated a restaurant in the back room of a saloon. I feel like a mole. I want this one to have lots of light and plants. I want a greenhouse."

C.J. debated with herself. It wasn't her problem. And Roarke Farrell certainly wouldn't welcome her assistance. Still, she stepped forward. "Maybe I can help."

"You?" Roarke stared at her in surprise.

"I couldn't help overhearing. I've had some experience with the Landmark Preservation Board."

"Can you talk some sense into them?" the woman asked. "Tell them we saved the Shelby Mansion. That should count for something. The other group of investors who wanted to buy it was going to tear it down and build a parking lot."

"What can you do?" Roarke asked.

"If I could use your phone?"

When he nodded, she lifted the receiver and punched in seven numbers. "Janet? This is C. J. Parker. Is Jerry free?" A moment later she continued, "Jerry, I need a favor. Not big. Just squeeze me on the agenda for your next meeting. Day after tomorrow? Fine. Ten minutes...I promise." C.J. laughed. "I'll tell you when I get there." As she replaced the phone, she spoke to the older woman. "I can't promise you anything except that I can present your side of the case."

C.J. found her hand grasped warmly. "I'm Gina Farrell, Roarke's mother. And you're—?"

"C. J. Parker. You can't be his mother."

Gina's delighted laugh filled the room. "I like you already. Do you work for Roarke?"

C.J. smiled. "Actually I work against him."

"That's even better. If you win this case for me, my son will owe you a favor."

C.J. shot Roarke an amused glance. "I'll be sure to collect. But I haven't won anything yet. I'll need to see the architect's drawings of the greenhouse, and I want to hear all about your plans for the restaurant."

"C'mon," Gina said, taking C.J.'s arm. "The plans are back at the restaurant. I'll tell you everything while you eat."

Roarke watched the two women leave. C. J. Parker puzzled him. No, puzzled was the wrong word. He rose and walked to the window, thinking of those two short moments when he'd come into physical contact with her, when she'd bumped up against him and when she'd taken his hand. Casual, brief contacts, both of them, and yet C. J. Parker had aroused more than his curiosity.

Why, he wondered as he directed his gaze to the street below and watched the two women emerge from the building. She certainly wasn't beautiful in any classic sense, not if you considered her features one by one. Yet somehow, combined the way they were . . .

He suddenly recalled the way he'd lost his train of thought when she'd smiled at him. Nothing like that had ever happened to him before.

By the time the two women reached the corner, his mother, as usual, was almost running, but Ms. Parker was easily keeping pace. Frowning thoughtfully, Roarke tried to remember the last time a woman had so completely captured his attention. His mother would say "never." She often complained that he'd spent his whole life devoted first to his sisters and her and now to his work.

He turned and let his gaze move around the room. Perhaps she was right. Being here in the District Attorney's office had been his dream for a long time. And it had required almost all of his time and energy. It was even more demanding now that his boss was retiring and, as acting D.A., he had a good chance of being elected to the position. Not that he didn't have room in his life for women. Not at all. But by necessity, he'd become an expert at keeping his relationships friendly, casual. He sat down in his chair. That was the way it had to be if he was going to clear some of these cases off of his desk.

With an unerring hand he reached for the file on Tony Williams again. It was an open-and-shut case. Such an easy conviction that Kevin Wilson, his self-appointed campaign manager, was urging him to try it himself. The resulting publicity would give his chances in the upcoming election a big boost.

But Rourke hadn't yet decided to follow Kevin's advice. He opened the file and searched for the notes he'd written at the time of the indictment. C. J. Parker had hit quite accurately on one of the major weaknesses of the case. Not one of the five witnesses had seen the blow being struck.

There was no reason to doubt that she would find and exploit the other weakness. No one had ever admitted to getting the bat out of the trunk of Tony's car. Both details had nagged at him from the very beginning. But he'd blamed whatever doubts he had about young Williams's guilt on his feeling of affinity for the boy. After all, they'd grown up in the same neighborhood and attended the same high school.

Roarke closed the file and looked around the room. What was he doing? He didn't have time to wonder how the bat got into Tony's hands, or why no one had seen Tony strike the blow. Danny's blood and Tony's fingerprints on the weapon would be more than enough evidence to convict. And mounting a good defense was Ms. Parker's job, not his.

Still . . . he recalled the fire in C.J.'s eyes when she'd rushed to her client's defense. She was convinced that Tony Williams was innocent. And when that kind of conviction was combined with the passion that he'd glimpsed in her, it would make her a formidable opponent in the courtroom.

He reached for the phone and punched in Kevin Wilson's number. It wouldn't hurt to find out more about C. J. Parker.

AT ONE-THIRTY ON FRIDAY, Roarke crossed the street to the Melrose Building. In half an hour C. J. Parker would be arguing his mother's case in front of the Landmark Preservation Board. There were any number of reasons why he should be present at the meeting. After all, he had a financial interest in the new building. And his mother was tied up at her restaurant. But he seldom indulged in self-deception. C. J. Parker had slipped into his mind too often during the past few days, and he was here to learn more about her.

Kevin's information had been minimal. After law school, she'd spent two years in the Chicago prosecutor's office. That didn't explain how she'd ended up in Syracuse sharing office space with Paul O'Shaughnessy. Paul was his friend and mentor. In the six months since the older man had undergone heart surgery, they'd met for dinner a few times, but not once had Paul mentioned his new associate.

Roarke spotted her when she was still a block away. There was a sensuous enjoyment to her stride that made him smile. Only a runner could get that kind of pleasure from merely walking.

As she drew nearer, he took in the other details of her appearance. Her hair was pulled back from her face, and she wore a prim navy suit and a white blouse. She carried no purse, just a briefcase that swung easily from her hand. The perfect costume, considering the conservative nature of the board members. O'Shaughnessy was training her well.

When she saw Roarke, C.J.'s free hand clenched into a fist.

"You don't look happy to see me," Roarke said.

She managed a smile. "I know how much this means to your mother, and I can understand that you might want to make the presentation yourself, but—"

"You're so eager to think the worst of me." He reached out and straightened the collar of her jacket. "Why is that?"

C.J. felt her pulse begin to race.

"Nice suit." With one finger, he smoothed the lapel.

She blinked, then stared at him with the faintest of frowns. She was keyed up because of the case. That had to be why she could hear her own heartbeat. She swallowed, then said, "You don't want to take over the case?"

"Why should I? My mother is very happy with you."

"Why are you here then?"

"I'm an investor in the Shelby. You could think of me as a client."

C.J. wrinkled her nose. "Lawyers make lousy clients."

He grinned. "True. Maybe it would be safer to think of me as a colleague. Who knows? I might even be able to help."

"The way you did with Judge Kaufmann? No, thanks."

"You got your postponement."

"For one month. I wanted two."

"Kaufmann's tough. I didn't think he'd give you more than two weeks."

"Ah, so that's why you so generously offered to agree to two weeks? You knew Kaufmann would give me that much for asking."

Roarke raised his hands, palms out. "How about a truce? Just for today?"

C.J. studied him for a moment. "As long as it's understood that I'm in charge of this case."

"I wouldn't have it any other way." He took her arm and led her up the steps of the Melrose Building. The gesture was automatic and meant to be impersonal. The fact that it wasn't had C.J.'s muscles tensing. Beneath the fabric of her jacket, she could feel the pressure of

each one of his fingers. Ridiculous, she thought as a revolving door gave her an excuse to break off contact
with him. She had almost succeeded in forgetting the
strange effect he'd had on her in his office. And now
this. Why was she reacting this way? Especially to this
man. She wasn't a silly schoolgirl.

As she led the way quickly across the lobby, she res-
olutely turned her thoughts to the strategy she'd
mapped out to handle the Landmark Preservation
Board. "Gina told me I could threaten your with-
drawal from the project."

"It's not merely a threat. We have a standing offer
from another group of investors to take the Shelby off
our hands."

"Yes, the parking lot people. I'm going to mention
them only as a last resort."

"Why? Won't the board see a greenhouse as the lesser
of two evils?"

"You'd think so, but the members of the Landmark
Board are volunteers, and they're idealists," C.J. continued as she stepped onto an escalator. "Margaret
Bushnell has raised three children, and now she's dedicated to saving our cultural heritage. Alice Downey is
a retired professor of English Literature who divides her
time between several women's activist groups and the
LPB. Jerry McDonald runs his own architectural firm.
At work, dollars and cents often have to prevail over
his love of beauty, but not when it comes to his decisions as a board member."

"You've certainly done your homework."

"Knowledge is strength." C.J. led the way off the es-
calators. "Don't get me wrong. These people do a fine
job."

"But . . ." Roarke said.

She sent him an amused look. "But sometimes their idealism blinds them, and they get carried away by their own power. You know, the 'I'd rather be right than be president' type. If the Shelby isn't going to be restored to the way it was in 1870, I almost think they'd rather see it destroyed."

"You're kidding."

She shook her head. "Don't worry, it won't come to that. I explained to Gina that there is a court of appeals, the City Planning Commission. There's not an idealist in the group, and they love anyone who promises to bring people, money and more collectible taxes downtown. The problem is they don't meet until the end of the month. If I can get the LPB to change its mind, the work on the Shelby can resume tomorrow."

"What's your plan?"

C.J.'s smile held more than a hint of mischief. "Just a little old-fashioned persuasion." She paused a few yards away from an open doorway. "We'd better enter separately."

When Roarke lifted his brows, her expression became serious, and she lowered her voice. "You're the acting D.A. They may recognize you. Most people don't bring a lawyer with them, and if they see two of us on one case, it could work against us."

"You figure all the angles, don't you?"

"I like to win. Why don't you sit near someone else? Talk to them, even if it's about the weather." She shrugged. "Anyone who happens to be looking will think you're their lawyer."

Roarke studied her for a minute. "You have this all planned out. Including how to get rid of me."

"We agreed that I'm in charge," C.J. said firmly.

"So we did." He turned and started for the door.

"What are you going to do?" C.J. asked.

"Even the best laid plans can sometimes be improved by a little improvisation."

With a great deal of effort, C.J. forced herself to count to twenty before she followed Roarke into the room. To her relief, she noted that he had taken a seat in the last row behind two men wearing work clothes. She didn't trust him and his ideas about improvising, but she didn't have time to worry about it. Jerry McDonald banged his gavel.

"Mr. and Mrs. Mitchell."

A young man rose and began to relate his tale of woe. Quickly C.J. scanned the room. The board members were seated at a long table in front of the windows. About thirty folding chairs were lined up in front of them, but only a few of them were filled. She sat as far away from Roarke as possible.

While young Mr. Mitchell rambled on with his rather long-winded complaint about an expensive chain-link fence he'd been asked to tear down, C.J. studied the faces of the board members. Margaret Bushnell wasn't even paying attention.

C.J. shifted in her chair to follow the direction of the woman's gaze. Roarke Farrell. Why wasn't she surprised? His rough-and-ready looks were enough to draw the attention of any woman, no matter what her age. But it was more than that. He had a certain magnetism. It made a woman wonder what it might be like if he... If he what? Improvised? She watched as Roarke leaned forward to speak to one of the men in front of him. At least he wasn't forgetting to play his role.

When she turned her attention back to the board, they were reaffirming the death sentence for the Mitchells's chain-link fence. If she had been arguing the case, she would have focused on the reason why the young couple had built the fence in the first place. To protect their home, their child, their dog, their whatever.

Jerry McDonald once more banged his gavel. "Mr. Lafferty, we'll hear your case now."

The man Roarke had spoken to earlier rose. "I'd like to request a ten-minute recess. I have to call my office."

After conferring with his colleagues, Jerry said, "Ms. Parker, since you need only ten minutes, why don't you take them while Mr. Lafferty makes his call?"

C.J. felt the familiar surge of adrenaline as she rose and smiled at the members of the board. "I'm here to ask you to revoke the work stoppage order on the Shelby Mansion. We all know that time is money, so I'm not going to bore you with the financial details. But I do want to tell you about Gina Farrell. I understand that you've all eaten at her restaurant on the north side." She paused long enough for Jerry and Alice to smile. "Mrs. Farrell wants to open a new place downtown, and she's always had this dream of having her restaurant in a greenhouse."

Turning, she opened her briefcase and removed three books. "The problem is that the Shelby Mansion did not have a greenhouse on its grounds in 1870. However, I have been able to locate some famous homes that did have what were called conservatories." She handed an open book to each of the board members.

"As you can see, Jefferson's conservatory at Monticello was attached to the south end of the house. Mark Twain's opened off the library. I don't have any pictures of the various ones that were added on the White House. The first one was built by Buchanan and the last one was torn down after the First World War."

At the back of the room, Roarke relaxed and began to enjoy himself. A little old-fashioned persuasion, she'd called it. Old or new, the first rule of a good argument was to appeal to the interests of the audience, and C.J. was doing just that. They wanted to save landmarks, and she was giving them a way to do that without violating their ideals.

O'Shaughnessy had gotten himself a damned fine associate. His train of thought was interrupted when Mr. Lafferty returned to his seat. Roarke leaned over and whispered, "Thanks."

"My pleasure. I'm getting paid by the hour to sit here and watch these birds flap their wings. I figure I don't have much chance of making them change their minds, but my boss wants me to go through the motions. How's your lady friend doing?"

"Two of the birds are eating out of her hand. That's a majority. Your boss might save some money if he hired her."

When C.J. began repacking her books, Roarke quietly left the room, but he lingered in the hall long enough to hear the board revoke their work stoppage order.

C.J. told herself that it wasn't disappointment she was feeling as she walked into the hall. Why would she be disappointed because Roarke had left? She hadn't wanted his help anyway. When she saw him waiting for her at the bottom of the escalator, she told herself she wasn't pleased. She smiled anyway.

"I'm impressed, Counselor," he said.

The quick surge of pleasure surprised her. "Thank you."

"No, I'm the one who should be thanking you. You saved my mother and the other investors including myself a lot of money."

C.J. brought her finger to her lips. "Shh." Then she glanced quickly over her shoulder. "Don't even mention the word. It doesn't carry much weight with the board members."

"So I noticed," he said, guiding her through the lobby and out the revolving door. She expected him to leave her then, but instead he fell into step beside her.

"The only thing I regret was that I didn't get to play a bigger role in your performance," he said.

"How did you get Lafferty to make that phone call?"

"I told him we had other plans for the afternoon."

When C.J. shot him a dark look, he shrugged. "I was improvising. Besides it worked. His boss may give you a call."

"For a hot date?"

"No, he needs some help with the LPB."

"Great. That's all I need. More clients who need me to argue in favor of fences or window moldings. Pretty soon I'll be the only person in my law school graduating class with a specialty in nineteenth century gazebos."

"Hey, what are colleagues for?"

C.J. was laughing when they reached her office building. As she climbed the first step, the sun haloed her hair, highlighting the reddish gold color. For a moment Roarke's mind emptied, and he simply stared.

"Roarke?"

"Hmm?"

"I asked if you wanted to tell Gina she can have her greenhouse?"

"You tell her." When she turned away, he said, "Have dinner with me. I'm a great cook."

"No, I—"

"Okay, we'll eat at your place."

"No. I can't—"

"Okay." Roarke sighed. "A restaurant then. Ordinarily I avoid them like the plague. But tonight I'll make an exception."

C.J. had to suppress a laugh. "I don't think it's a good idea. We're opponents on the Williams case."

Roarke's eyebrows rose. "We won't discuss it."

She shook her head. "It's not just the case. I have this rule. I don't go out with other lawyers."

"Okay, think of me as a client then. If I were Gina, you wouldn't turn me down."

C.J. hesitated, surprised at how much she was tempted to say yes. How long had it been since she'd enjoyed the simple pleasure of celebrating a victory with a colleague? Or going out on a date with a man, for that matter? Not since she'd come to Syracuse. But was it the idea of celebrating her victory that appealed or was it simply the man? Ignoring the little warning voice in her head, she said, "Okay. But you'll have to settle for a drink, not dinner. I have a lot of work to catch up on."

"I'll meet you here at five-thirty." He waited until she disappeared through the doors of the building.

3

It was almost an hour later when C.J. led Roarke through the crowd at Patsy's Pub. In the far corner of the room, a television set hung from the ceiling, its volume drowned out by laughter and voices. The air smelled of cigarette smoke, beer and people. C.J. drew in a deep breath and tried to relax. She'd purposely chosen a place where she'd be surrounded by people she knew. Several of them waved or shouted a greeting as she threaded her way with practiced ease to the bar. The sandy-haired bartender gave her his immediate attention.

"How'd the case go?" he asked.

"Very well." C.J. blew him a quick kiss. "Thanks to those books you dug up." She turned to Roarke and pitched her voice to be heard. "Meet Sid. He and his brother Doug own this place. But his day job is in the research department of the college library. He's the one who found all those lovely pictures of nineteenth-century greenhouses for me."

Sid shook Roarke's hand. "Congratulations. I put a bottle of champagne on ice." He produced a bucket from under the counter and handed it to Roarke. "It's on the house."

"You don't have to do that," C.J. said.

"It's a bribe," Sid explained with a grin. "Doug wanted to make sure you were in a good mood. He sprained his ankle, so we're going to need you after all in the Charity Run. You've got three and a half weeks to train. Practice is on Sunday at nine."

Before C.J. could say a word, Sid had disappeared around the corner of the horseshoe-shaped bar. "Dammit," she muttered.

Roarke looked at her in amusement. "It's French if that's any consolation."

She glanced up at him.

"The champagne. It's expensive."

She made a face. "I'm going to pay dearly for it."

"The run's only ten kilometers. What's the problem?"

"The problem is that I'll finish last. Sid and Doug want to win. They figure that the publicity will be good for Patsy's Pub. And they have this mistaken idea that I'm fast."

"And you're not?"

"I'm like the tortoise who raced with the hare. All stamina and no speed." She sighed. "No matter. I'll just have to find someone to take my place. Right after I kick Doug in his good ankle. I'm sure he's faking." She led the way to an adjacent room and chose a table next to a solid wall of windows facing the street. Outside, pedestrians hurried along the sidewalk, separated from them by only a half inch of glass.

While Roarke tipped champagne into two glasses, C.J. gave him a speculative look. "I don't suppose I could persuade you to run for me?"

"I'm already committed to run for the D.A.'s office. We won the race last year, and we plan to keep the trophy. However, I'd be happy to offer my services as a personal coach."

"I just bet you would. That would give you an opportunity to sabotage the competition."

Roarke sighed. "I can see you're determined to think the worst of me. I was just offering to help out."

She felt the bubble of laughter begin to rise and managed to control it. "Right. But it would be a hopeless task. I'll never be fast. My legs are too short."

"With the proper coaching, leg length is not a factor."

C.J.'s eyebrows rose. "And I suppose you've gathered evidence to support that theory?"

Roarke shrugged and handed her a glass of champagne. "Look at that tiny woman from Portugal who wins all the marathons. Or Joan Benoit in the eighty-four Olympics."

"They're professional athletes. They run hundreds of miles every week. They probably exist on a diet of raw spinach and tofu." C.J. shuddered. "I'd rather be hung by my thumbs."

"If you're determined to misinterpret everything I say..."

This time the bubble of laughter escaped. Roarke Farrell was not what she expected. Lit with amusement, his eyes were the color of smoke. And where there was smoke... Quite suddenly she felt out of breath, as if she had just finished a ten-kilometer race.

Outside the window, a whistle shrilled as a policeman directed the flow of rush-hour traffic. The noise broke the spell. C.J. sipped her champagne, welcoming the icy taste as it slid down her throat. She glanced out at the street. A couple walked by, so close she could have touched them if it hadn't been for the window.

She'd brought Roarke here, hoping that in familiar surroundings she could figure out a way to handle the feelings he stirred in her. Normally she had no trouble keeping men at arm's length. And even with the few that she'd allowed to get closer, she'd never completely let down her guard. Not even with Brad Whitney. Thank heavens for that. Remembering the man she'd dated briefly in Chicago still hurt. A talented and ambitious attorney, he was not unlike the man sitting across from her right now. He, too, had tempted her to bend her rule about not dating lawyers. And the price she'd paid for it . . .

Suddenly she realized that she was no longer looking at the passersby, but at Roarke's reflection in the glass. As she watched his hand reach for the champagne and his fingers close around the bottle, she remembered the strength of that hand and the pressure of each one of those fingers against her arm when he had guided her into the Melrose Building. With a frown, she returned her gaze to the reflection of his face. She couldn't allow herself to forget that he was a prosecutor, and an ambitious one. Hadn't she learned her lesson with Brad?

Roarke was too interested in C.J. to pay much attention to the pedestrians outside the window. Her choice of a bar where she had friends amused him. So did her selection of this particular table. They might as well have been drinking champagne in a fishbowl. Clearly she did not want to be alone with him. Still, the reason for her reluctance intrigued him. Was it personal, or simply because of her rule about lawyers? Or did it have something to do with Paul O'Shaughnessy? Only the latter possibility bothered him.

"Tell me. Why don't you go out with lawyers?"

"They argue too much, and they're not happy unless they win."

The answer had come quickly, Roarke noted. Too quickly. He smiled. "Obviously, you've dated the wrong one."

Her lips curved, but he saw the quick flash of pain in her eyes before she dropped her gaze to the wineglass. He reached out to cover her hand with his. "I'm sorry. I didn't mean to stir up a bad memory."

Kindness. She hadn't expected it from him. Nor could she have anticipated the sudden urge to tell him what had happened in Chicago. She'd never told anyone. Pushing it out of her mind, she said, "My parents were both attorneys."

She hadn't meant to say that, either. She studied Roarke over the rim of her wineglass. He had an amazing ability to become perfectly still. She'd often seen her father do the same thing in a courtroom, encouraging a witness to pour out his story. Kind or not, Roarke Farrell was a dangerous man. She removed her hand from beneath his. "They argued all the time, and they both wanted to win. The marriage ended in divorce."

There was hurt there, too, Roarke decided. But it was too soon to probe. He sipped his wine and leaned back in his chair. The more he learned about C. J. Parker, the more questions he had. "Why did you take the Tony Williams case?"

C.J. frowned. "We agreed not to discuss that."

He waved her objection aside. "There's nothing improper about my question, and you know it."

C.J. ran her finger up the stem of her wineglass. How could she possibly explain why she took the case? Because of the look in a mother's eyes? Because of the way a boy ran on the track? She met Roarke's eyes again. "Paul asked me the same thing. I believe the boy is innocent."

It was Roarke's turn to frown. "Why would Paul ask you that? Didn't he refer the case to you?"

C.J. smiled. "Hardly. He'd prefer that I didn't practice criminal law at all." Noticing Roarke's surprised expression, she hurried on. "Now, it's my turn for a question. Your office was very aggressive in prosecuting this case. What if Tony had been the victim and Danny Jasper had used the bat? Would you still have brought a charge of first-degree assault against the upstanding young college student?"

"You can bet on it," Roarke replied.

"In spite of the pressure of the college and the boy's influential parents?"

Roarke studied C.J. He might have taken offense if the cynicism in her tone hadn't contrasted so sharply with the emotion in her eyes. As it was, he smiled. "I like to put the bad guys in jail, no matter who they are." He remembered then that she'd worked for the District Attorney's office in Chicago. "You don't think much of prosecutors, do you?"

"No." She sipped her wine.

"Obviously your experience has been limited. When you get to know me better, your opinion of us will improve."

C.J. choked, nearly spilling the rest of her drink. Then she shot him a withering glance. "I'm already impressed by the size of your ego!"

Roarke threw back his head and laughed. The sound was rich, unbridled. C.J. found herself smiling in response. Outside, the traffic had thinned, and the policeman climbed into his car. At the bar, someone began to sing.

Roarke watched the last rays of sunlight slant through the window and set the ends of C.J.'s hair on fire. His fingers itched to reach out and touch. When she lifted her glass, he caught the gleam of gems on her wrist.

This time he gave in to the impulse and captured her hand to lift it and examine the bracelet. A fine, gold chain linked three sapphires, each flanked by a small diamond. Expensive but dainty, it might have been designed especially for her slender wrist. Someone had taken care in the selection. Who?

"A gift from an admirer?" he asked.

C.J.'s eyes were on their joined hands. His skin was dark against hers, his fingers slightly callused. When they brushed against the veins on her wrist, she felt her pulse skip a beat and begin to race. The glint of satisfaction in his eyes told her that he felt it, too. She fought the urge to pull her hand away. When his lips curved in a smile, her gaze shifted to his mouth. His lips were full and sensual. With very little effort she could imagine how they would feel pressed against hers.

Her eyes were so clear. He could read every thought, every feeling. Desire moved through him settling hot and hard in his center. His fingers tightened on her wrist to tug her closer, and the bracelet pressed into his skin. His gaze dropped to it.

"Who gave you this?" he asked.

"My—" She caught herself just in time. "Paul gave it to me."

At his look of surprise, she hurried on. "When I graduated from law school."

"You've known him for a while then?"

"Yes. He went to law school with my mother."

"I see. Then he knew both of your parents."

C.J. nodded, but her fingers had tightened on the stem of the glass. It was a simple enough explanation. Why was he so sure there was a more complicated one? What exactly was he trying to find out anyway? That his old friend was having an affair with a woman young enough to be his daughter? Impossible. A man Paul's age, a man who'd had a recent brush with death? Perhaps not so impossible. Roarke was considering how to press her further when he heard music, faint but unmistakable, above the noise of the bar. He twisted in his chair to locate the source. "A band?"

"It's coming from the upper level room," C.J. explained. "Sid's idea. Doug's against it. It cuts into the dining space. But Sid maintains that they have to lure the customers in before they can hope to feed them."

"Why don't we try it out? Then we can offer them an objective opinion."

She was surprised that she wanted to say "Yes." The second surprise came when she tried to reach for her glass and found that Roarke still had her hand. Drawing it away, she said, "I can't. I have a lot of work—"

"You can't dance."

"Yes, I can. I don't—"

"It's the music, isn't it? That South American beat scares you off, I'll bet."

C.J. concentrated on the sound for a minute. He was right. The band was playing a rumba or something.

"Most women just don't have enough confidence to try something that tricky."

"Most women?" C.J. rose from her chair. "I can dance to that if you can." She led the way to the dance floor. Just as Roarke drew her into his arms, she pulled back. "I'm going to figure out how you do that, and then it's not going to work."

"Do what?" Roarke asked innocently.

Her eyes narrowed. "Talk me into doing things I have no intention of doing."

"It's my charm."

She gave an unladylike snort as they began to move to the music. "Dream on. You switch topics in the middle of a discussion. That's what you do. You ask me to dinner, and I refuse. Then somehow Gina's name pops up, and I end up offering to buy you a drink."

"Sid paid for the drinks," he reminded her.

"Shut up. Next I refuse to dance with you, and suddenly I'm out here standing up for the whole sisterhood of women."

"Pay attention to the music," he warned as he swung her out and pulled her back into his arms.

She resisted his next move. "One dance, Farrell. Then I'm leaving. Case closed. And you have no chance of an appeal."

He grinned down at her. "If court's no longer in session, why don't you relax and concentrate on the music?"

Much to her surprise, she did just that. Later she would ask herself why she'd let down her guard. Perhaps it was because of the champagne. Or perhaps it was because he didn't try to hold her too close. But it felt so good to relax and let the music and the movement of his body guide her. It had been so long since she'd simply enjoyed being held by a man. Maybe too long. She rested her cheek against his shoulder.

For a while they didn't speak. He kept the steps simple at first, using only body language to communicate what he wanted her to do. A press of his hand at her waist, a brush of his thigh against hers, and her body seemed to move instinctively with his. When he ran his fingers lightly up her back, she relaxed even more and drew in his scent. He smelled different. Good.

She fit nicely in his arms, Roarke thought as he guided her around the edge of the small dance floor. Her hair just brushed against his chin, and a faint flowery scent drifted up to him. How long had it been since he'd had the time to take a woman dancing? He'd almost forgotten how good it felt to hold a woman in his arms and flow with the music.

"This is nice," C.J. murmured.

"Umm." Although he could have wished for more privacy—an empty room with dimmer lights and slower, softer music. As he drew her closer, the image grew sharper in his mind. Suddenly he thought of Paul. Did she dance this way with him?

"I haven't danced in such a long time," C.J. said.

Had she read his thoughts? "Why not?"

"Too busy. You must know how it is. Law school is such a rat race. There's no time to do anything but think about the next paper, the next exam. Then you get out, and there's no time to do anything except deal with the next client, the next case."

"Kevin mentioned that you worked for a couple of years in Chicago in the D.A.'s office. How did you end up in Syracuse?"

"I always intended to come here. I took the job offer in Chicago because I needed trial experience. I plan to be Paul's partner someday."

"Indeed."

As the music ended, Roarke circled her waist with his arm and urged her backward into a dip. She was laughing when he pulled her up. "Where did you learn to dance?"

"My mother taught me," he explained as he led her back to their table. "She considered it an essential aspect of her children's education. I got more than my share of practice partnering my two sisters."

When Roarke pulled out her chair, C.J. remained standing. "I'm leaving, remember?"

He lifted the champagne bottle out of the ice. "It's a shame to waste it."

She covered her glass with her hand.

"You still have a swallow left," he pointed out. "And we haven't made a toast yet."

Half amused, half exasperated, C.J. lifted her glass. "Do you ever give up?"

"Never. To our future...associations. May they all be as pleasant as today's."

She met his eyes squarely. "To your rich fantasy life."

His laugh was quick and spontaneous. She had to bite the side of her cheek to keep from joining him. Instead she drained her glass and set it on the table. "Face it, Farrell. Today's as pleasant as it's going to get. When we meet again, it will be strictly business, and we'll be on opposite sides."

"I always enjoy going up against a worthy opponent," Roarke replied as he took her arm and cleared a path to the door.

Outside, the sky was still holding on to some light, and the air carried the lingering scent of exhaust fumes. C.J. breathed it in, enjoying the unmistakable smell of the city.

"I'll see you to your car," Roarke said.

"I walked to work."

"I'll drive you home then."

C.J. smiled. "It'll be a short trip." She took a few steps to a recessed, glass-paneled door. Roarke noted the lettering, Old Erie Gallery.

"You live in an art gallery?"

She laughed as she opened the door. "Those were my . . . Paul's exact words when I brought him here the first time. My apartment's above the restaurant." But when she turned to him in the narrow foyer, she saw that he wasn't amused.

"O'Shaughnessy can't approve of your living here." His tone was sarcastic.

"Perhaps he doesn't. It's really none of his business."

Roarke ignored the implication in the words she left unsaid. "This is not the safest neighborhood." He tapped on the glass in the door. "A nitwit could break through this."

C.J. tightened the rein on her temper. "I'll have to remember that the next time I lock myself out." She turned on her heel and marched up the stairs. She was looking into security systems, but she'd bite her tongue off before she told him.

Roarke wanted to shake her. How many times had she brought Paul here, he wondered. He dogged her steps to the second floor.

C.J. concentrated on ignoring him while she inserted her key into the lock. It stuck, and she swore under her breath while she jiggled it. Roarke Farrell was overbearing and overprotective. But he was not going to make her lose her temper. When he strode past her to the fire-escape window at the end of the hall, she began to count to ten. On three, she heard the scrape of metal and his muttered curse. On five, he stormed back to her and grabbed her shoulder to spin her around.

His fury was almost tangible. She took one quick step backward into the wall.

"I accepted your explanation for meeting your client the other day at the track. We all take a risk now and then if the reason is sufficient. But there's no excuse for this kind of carelessness." He reached for her hand, and dropped a rusty window latch into it.

Her fingers closed tightly around the metal. "You have no right, no right at all to lecture me."

"Anyone has the right to lecture a fool."

Her fist connected with his stomach, and she had the satisfaction of hearing his pained grunt before both her wrists were trapped in his hands.

She didn't struggle. Timing was everything. Keeping her eyes steady on his, she said, "I'm not one of your sisters."

"Thank God."

Her leg moved then, but he caught it neatly between his. Then he leaned forward, pressing her flat against the wall.

Anger. That was the reason for the flash of heat racing through her veins. It was her own temper flaring to match his. She might have even believed it, but she couldn't speak. Words, always her best defense, had slipped beyond her reach. He was so close. Then suddenly he was even closer, his body in full contact with hers. She didn't move, not a muscle. But every inch of her was aware of the hard length of his thigh, the sharp angle of his hip and the quick beat of his heart. Or was it hers?

Even in the dim hallway, Roarke could see the anger drain from her eyes. His own disappeared with it, leaving something else, just as potent. He wanted her. Perhaps he had wanted her from the first. His eyes moved to her lips. They were parted, waiting. He could feel the pulse at her wrist, racing as fast as his own. For an instant, he thought of making love to her right there in the hallway. He could picture the way her skin would look in the muted light, the way her hair would look falling around her shoulders. He could almost feel it brushing against his skin. The strength of the image, so tempting, so outrageous, stunned him. He hadn't even kissed her. What was it about her that could take him this far, this fast? What would happen if he did kiss her? Very slowly, he drew back and released her hands. A wise man took precautions before playing with fire.

C.J. struggled to clear her mind. An instant ago her skin had burned. Now it felt like ice. What had just happened? What had he done to her? Nothing, really. He hadn't even kissed her. But for one shivery moment she had wanted him to. The thought brought instant clarity to her mind and strength to her voice. "Get out of here!"

Roarke backed away two steps. "Lock your door." He was smiling when he turned and walked away.

C.J. didn't move until she heard the outer door close. Only then did she attempt to walk into her apartment. After slamming the door, she found she was still holding the rusted window latch in her hand. With an oath, she hurled it at the couch.

4

ROARKE STOPPED SHORT the moment he stepped out of the elevator. Ahead of him at the door of Judge Burgan's courtroom, C. J. Parker was talking to Paul O'Shaughnessy. He watched her laugh and lean closer to hear something Paul said. Then she placed her hand on his shoulder and rose on tiptoe to kiss his cheek.

Before either of them could glance his way, Roarke turned and walked away from the cozy scene. At the end of the corridor, he stopped to stare out a window.

There was no need to analyze what he was feeling. He'd had all weekend to do that. But recognizing jealousy was a lot easier than controlling it or even understanding it.

His thoughts drifted back to Friday night, to those few minutes in the hallway outside of her apartment. He'd handled that badly. Helping to raise his two sisters had taught him the value of subtlety.

A quick laugh escaped as he recalled his first meeting with C.J. There'd been nothing subtle about his approach that time. Nor had there been anything subtle about his desire to make love to her on the floor outside her apartment. And he hadn't even kissed her. No other woman had ever made him want that desperately, that quickly.

But then C.J. wasn't like any other woman he had ever dated. Not one of them had had that fiery passion simmering just below the surface. His lips curved. Was that the attraction? He was certainly tempted to find out what it might be like to set it loose. A different man, a wiser man would give C. J. Parker a wide berth. But he had learned a long time ago to take advantage of the unexpected surprises that life put in his path.

Unless she was involved with Paul. He paced to the other side of the hallway and back to the window. But what evidence did he have to support that? C.J. had given Paul a kiss on the cheek. He'd gone to law school with her mother. That made him an old friend of the family, didn't it? Or were they both hiding something?

With a sigh, Roarke stopped pacing and leaned against the window. C.J. definitely had a way of making him overreact. It was useless to speculate. He didn't have enough facts, and there was only one way to get them. He and Paul hadn't gotten together for dinner in much too long.

Glancing at his watch, he swore and hurried down the hall. He'd come within two minutes of being late. Judge Bergan was hearing the preliminary motions on the Sandra Hughes trial, and she had little tolerance for tardy lawyers.

C.J. BOUGHT two turkey dogs from a vendor and sat on one of the stone benches outside the courthouse. The April sunshine was luring people out of their office buildings for lunch.

"Where did you disappear to?" Paul asked as he sat down next to her. "I wanted to introduce you to Roarke Farrell."

"We've met," C.J. said.

He gave her a surprised look. "You never mentioned it."

"It must have slipped my mind." C.J. handed him a hot dog and hoped that lightning wouldn't strike her dead. For three days and nights she had prayed for Roarke Farrell to slip her mind. So far her prayers hadn't been answered.

Paul looked at his lunch with distaste. "It looks naked without chili."

"Close your eyes," C.J. suggested. In spite of his complaints and his passion for chili dogs, Paul had been watching his diet since his open-heart surgery. "Cheer up, I'm bringing steaks for dinner on Friday. Or have you forgotten?"

"Fat chance. It's the only way I can choke down those bran muffins every morning." He took a tentative bite of his hot dog and made a face while he chewed and swallowed. "What did you think of the way Roarke Farrell put me through my paces?"

"As a lawyer, he reminds me a lot of you."

Paul laughed. "I knew you'd like him. He'll keep you on your toes during the Williams trial."

C.J. stared at her father. "What do you mean?"

Paul tossed the rest of his lunch into a nearby trash can. "The District Attorney's sick leave is permanent and Roarke has been asked to run for election in the fall. He just told me that he's being pressured to supervise the Sandra Hughes trial and handle the Williams case in person." Whatever else Paul would have said was interrupted by a reporter wielding a microphone. She was shadowed by a jeans-clad young man with a television camera on his shoulder.

"Mr. O'Shaughnessy, I'm Suzie Miller with Channel Two News. Any comments on the preliminary motions in the Hughes trial?"

"No comment." Paul softened his refusal with a smile. "You might better talk to my learned opponent from the District Attorney's office. And speak of the devil . . ." Paul gestured toward the courthouse door. "Here he comes."

Roarke made it halfway down the steps before the microphone was thrust into his face. He was too far away for C.J. to catch what he was saying. Still, she could feel the potent warmth of his smile when he aimed it at the TV camera. She turned back to her father. "What does the election have to do with which trial Roarke handles?"

"A murder trial is always high profile. But in the Hughes case, we have the added drama of a scorned woman accused of murdering her lover, who just happened to be very rich and very married. The press is going to go into a feeding frenzy." Grinning, he waved a hand at Suzie Miller who was still managing to block Roarke's path. "It's starting already. Covering preliminary motions is about as interesting as watching grass grow."

C.J. was puzzled. "I would think that it's just the kind of case that Roarke would want to prosecute."

"Sure. But what if he doesn't win it? The election is only six months away, and a loss could seriously damage his chances. On the other hand, the Williams trial will generate a lot of publicity, too. It involves young people and the safety of our city streets. A conviction is almost guaranteed, and Roarke Farrell will become an instant hero."

"So my client gets caught up in the public relations blitz of an election year. It's not fair."

Paul looked amused. "No one ever said it was. You have to have a strong stomach to—"

"Please, not another lecture." She glanced over at Roarke. Suzie Miller was hanging on his every word. How could she have forgotten for a minute that he was a prosecutor? Worse still, why had she allowed herself to hope, even for a minute, that he might be different, that he might not value winning over everything else? In a determined voice, she said, "Convicting Tony won't be as easy as he thinks."

"Big talk. Any progress with your Perry Mason strategy?"

"Not so far. But Sam Hillerman thinks he'll have something for me later in the week. So far I haven't had any luck getting an interview with the victim, Danny Jasper. I'm beginning to wonder if they're hiding something."

Paul grinned. "You've inherited my suspicious mind." He rose and dusted off his pants. "I want to ask Roarke something."

"I'll catch up with you later." C.J. deposited her hot dog into a nearby trash can. When she turned around, she found her path blocked by Suzie Miller and her camera-toting sidekick.

"Ms. Parker, Mr. Farrell has just informed us that you are Tony Williams's new attorney, and that you've already pulled some legal hocus-pocus to arrange for a postponement of justice for your client. Our noontime audience would like to know why."

Several responses flashed into C.J.'s mind. Over Suzie Miller's shoulder she saw Roarke give her a two-fingered salute. Quite suddenly the humor of the situation struck her. After all, Paul had sicced the press on him. Turnabout was fair play. She smiled into the camera and said, "No comment."

THE HALF-HOUR RIDE to her father's home in the country usually took C.J.'s mind off her troubles. During the winter, the steep hills and icy roads had required all of her concentration. But spring in Syracuse didn't offer much in the way of distraction. A week of sunshine had melted the snow, but the trees were still bare, the fields brown. The landscape reminded her of the week she'd put in, and even with the top down and a Billy Joel song blasting out of her tape deck, she was having a hard time relaxing.

On Monday night, she'd been portrayed on the news as a villain, thanks to Roarke Farrell. Scowling, she eased her foot off the gas pedal as her Volkswagen sailed around a curve. Strictly speaking, Roarke was not to blame for the rumpus raised by the press over the postponement, but there were plenty of other things she could lay at his door. Like the fact that she still could not walk down the hall to her apartment without recalling those few moments of shivering intensity between them. C.J. bit her lip and for the second time in as many minutes lifted her foot off the gas pedal. Damn the man! He was even interfering with her driving.

In desperation, she began to sing along with Billy Joel, and by the time she pulled into Paul's driveway, she was almost on-key.

She grabbed the bag of steaks and wine that Sid had loaded into her back seat and carried it up the front steps. The door was ajar. How like her father to forget to close it. Kicking it open, she stepped into the foyer.

Something smelled wonderful. Garlic she could recognize, but there were other, more elusive scents that had her mouth watering as she followed her nose to the kitchen. Paul's culinary talents were pretty much limited to opening cans.

But it wasn't her father that she found chopping vegetables at the island work space in the center of the room.

"You." They both spoke at once. C.J. simply stared as Roarke moved toward her to take the bag. He looked different with a towel tucked into low-slung jeans. More threatening. The black T-shirt did nothing to hide the well-developed muscles of his shoulders and upper arms.

One glance at her face had Roarke grinning as he made room on the table for the bag. He'd been just as surprised as she. Paul hadn't mentioned that C.J. would be joining them when they'd made their plans to have dinner. But handling the unexpected was one of the skills he'd picked up over the years. And hadn't he come to find out more about C. J. Parker? His grin widened as he turned back to her. "You're always so happy to see me."

"What are you doing here?"

He gestured toward the work island. "I'm making dinner."

"So am I. Steaks." She lifted a package out of the bag and carried it to the refrigerator. "And I only brought two."

"Pasta can always be stretched. I'll share if you will."

For the first time C.J. took in the cluttered condition of the kitchen. Bags and boxes covered every inch of counter space. There were even a few on the floor. It made her think of his office. The man had a definite knack for creating chaos. "Where's Paul?" she asked.

"He's running an errand." Roarke fished a skillet out of a bag and set it over a low flame. "He left a note on the door and a key under the mat."

C.J. watched him add oil and vegetables to the pan while she considered her dwindling options. Leaving was out. There was no way she was going to run away from Roarke Farrell, and it would take a moving van to get rid of him. Her eyes widened when he lifted a food processor out of a box. "Do you always bring your own equipment when you come to dinner?"

"Have you ever eaten one of Paul's meals?"

C.J. grinned. "I've sworn off." She selected a bottle of wine from her bag and crossed to the island. "What are you making?"

"Sauce for pasta with fresh tomatoes, garlic and basil." He gave the pan a toss. C.J.'s mouth began to water. "You did say something about sharing?" she asked.

He gave her a considering look. "Make me an offer."

"One-third of my steak. Sid orders it special for Patsy's."

Roarke stirred the contents of the pan and waved some of the steam in her direction. She made the mistake of breathing it in. Heaven. "Half of my steak."

"Here, taste." She opened her mouth and closed her eyes, letting the flavors blossom on her tongue for as long as she dared. Even as she swallowed, her hunger grew.

"I learned to make this at my mother's knee, and she learned how to make it from her mother. For two-thirds of your steak, I'll give you the recipe."

C.J. opened her eyes and met Roarke's. They were filled with laughter. Her fingers tightened on the wine bottle she was still holding. She placed it on the counter between them. "Half of my steak and half of the bottle of wine."

He picked it up and inspected the label. "You have a deal, Counselor. Why don't we drink to it?" He produced a corkscrew out of yet another bag. "Out of my half, of course."

As they laughed, their eyes met and held once more. C.J. felt a jolt all the way down to her toes. This time he wasn't even touching her. What was it about him? If she could find out, perhaps she could handle it.

Roarke kept his eyes on the wine bottle as he uncorked it and poured. Why was it that a moment of shared laughter could make him forget why he had come here tonight? He placed one of the glasses in front of her, then lifted his and swirled the contents around. The aroma was sharp, inviting, not unlike the woman sitting across from him. The silky lemon-colored blouse she wore made him think of spring sunshine. The kind that had always tempted him to cut classes and play hooky. With her hair loose and tossed by the wind, she looked like a teenager, much too young to be involved with a man Paul's age. For a moment his fingers tightened on the stem of his glass. He willed them to relax. Then he raised his glass and waited. This time when they met his, her eyes held a mixture of wariness and curiosity. Or was he merely seeing a reflection of his own feelings?

C.J. smiled and spoke first. "To our meal-sharing bargain."

"How about a toast to your brief but stunning career on the nightly news?" Then he watched in surprise as the smile faded from her eyes. "What's wrong?"

"Nothing."

When he waited patiently, saying nothing, she shrugged. "Nothing really. Just a crank phone call."

"When did you get it?"

"On Monday around midnight. They replayed Suzie Miller's tape on the eleven o'clock news." She took a sip of her wine and set it on the counter. "Usually I would have my answering machine on at that hour, but I thought it might be Paul, that he might be calling to make some joke." She folded her hands together on her lap. "I shouldn't have answered it."

"A man?"

"Yes."

"What did he say?"

"Not much that I care to remember." When Roarke said nothing, she continued. "He wanted me to drop Tony's case."

Roarke pictured her alone in her apartment, listening to threats in the middle of the night. The quick swallow of wine did nothing to cool his fury. "What did Paul say?"

"Nothing. I don't want him to know." She slid from the stool and faced him squarely across the counter. "He's getting more than his share of stress handling the Hughes case. Besides, it was the kind of thing a kid would do. Calling someone at midnight. And I don't need another lecture."

Roarke set his glass down quickly. "Whoa. Slow down. I guess I can understand why you didn't tell him. And the last thing I want to do is blow it out of proportion. But if it happens again, you should talk to someone about it."

"Why?"

"Because it helps." He smiled. "I have a whole drawerful of hate mail at home so I speak from experience."

C.J. studied him for a minute. Why did it always surprise her that he was kind? She leaned her elbows on the counter. "A whole drawerful?"

"You don't believe me?"

"I would have guessed a roomful."

Roarke grinned. "I only keep the best ones. You could come to my apartment tonight after dinner. I'll read you a few."

Her laugh bubbled up. "What an original line. Do you have much success with it?"

"I'm not sure. Do I?"

His eyes held mischief and a definite challenge. But some risks were best avoided. C.J. shook her head. "It doesn't sound very romantic to me." She picked up her glass, and his fingers closed around hers to hold it steady while he poured more wine.

"You're looking for romance then?"

"No." She tried very hard to ignore the ribbon of warmth that curled up her arm. Very carefully she drew her hand from his grasp. "I don't have time for romance."

Roarke nodded. "Ah, yes. I forgot. You're too busy becoming Paul's partner." He stooped to lift a shiny machine out of one of the bags and clamped it to the edge of the counter. "I'd say you've made a good start.

He's never hired anyone to work for him before. You have the inside track."

"If I become his partner, it will be because I earn it and not because I have an inside track." C.J.'s voice was controlled, but the look she aimed at him had enough fire in it to singe his skin.

Roarke gave the glass she still held in her hand a wary glance, then raised his hands in surrender. "No offense intended. I'd prefer not to end up wearing that wine."

When she set the glass on the counter, he said, "How about helping me make pasta?"

"I thought it came out of a box."

"Store-bought is nothing at all like the real thing. Could you grab the eggs? They're in one of those bags over there."

By the time C.J. delivered the carton, Roarke was measuring flour into the food processor. With skilled and graceful movements, he broke eggs and pushed buttons. "Thanks to the miracle of modern machinery, this doesn't take much longer than opening a box," he explained, dribbling water through the tube. Within seconds a ball of dough formed. C.J. watched in wonder as he lifted it out of the bowl and flattened it on a board.

"That's it?"

"Not quite. It has to rest a few minutes. Otherwise it has the elasticity of a rubber band. Then all we have to do is crank it through the machine a few times."

She gave the ball of dough a tentative poke. "Opening a box is easier."

"Wait'll you taste."

She sipped her wine. "When did you learn to cook?"

He disassembled the food processor and began to rinse it in the sink. "My mother opened her restaurant when I was eighteen, and my sisters and I were immediately drafted to work in the kitchen. We could either learn to cook or wash dishes. It didn't take me long to opt for becoming a chef."

C.J. tried to picture it in her mind. It sounded warm and cozy, a family working together, something she'd dreamed of as a child. "It sounds like fun."

Roarke recalled the steaming pots, demanding customers, endless hours of repeating the same tasks. But there'd been laughter and closeness. He turned and leaned against the sink. "I suppose you could call it fun if you enjoy hysteria and chaos. What about you? When did you learn how to cook?"

"I didn't."

His brows lifted. "How did you manage that?"

"I lived with my grandparents when I wasn't away at school. They had a French chef. Very temperamental. No one was allowed in his kingdom."

"You and Paul must make quite a pair in the kitchen." It was not a happy thought.

"I can make coffee and grill steaks."

"Caffeine and red meat?"

C.J. waved a hand at him. "I live over a restaurant, remember? Sid and Doug see to it that I get plenty of fruits and veggies." She wrinkled her nose. "Even sprouts."

He hadn't forgotten her living arrangements, nor a plan he'd thought of to make them safer. Slicing a piece of dough off the ball, he began to feed it between the rollers on the machine. "Want to help?"

"Sure." She moved around the counter as he stepped back to make room for her.

"Take the handle and turn."

It was easier said than done, C.J. discovered. She had to throw her whole weight into it, but gradually the ball of dough was transformed into a wide, flat ribbon. To her disappointment, Roarke folded it into a square, adjusted the rollers and began to feed it between them again. They repeated the process three times until the dough became thin and almost endless. This time Roarke had to reach around her to catch the pasta and loop it through his hands.

It was only as his body brushed against hers that she realized how close he was. She turned and found herself trapped against the counter. His arms caged her in on either side. Panic bubbled up. "You'll have to move," she said.

"Can't. I'm tied up at the moment."

Glancing over her shoulder, she saw that his hands were indeed handcuffed in pasta. Her pulse began to race as she tried to think of a way to get free. Any move she made would bring her body into full contact with his. The memory of what that would feel like came flooding back, sending an arrow of heat up her spine. Suddenly breathless, she took a deep breath. Big mistake, she realized as she drew in his scent. It was an even bigger mistake to look at his mouth, only inches away. Worse still to look into his eyes. They had darkened, and she could see herself trapped in their smoky depths.

It was happening again, Roarke thought as desire flared, then tightened in his center. This close, he could see the pulse that hammered where her blouse opened to reveal the delicate line of her throat. For a week he'd been wondering what it would be like to kiss her. To taste her. Now, only inches away, her lips were parted, moist. It was time to find out. Slowly he leaned forward and gently slipped the pasta off his wrists and onto the counter.

Wide-eyed, C.J. clasped the handle of a drawer behind her and braced herself. But her defenses began to crumble the moment she felt the heat of his breath on her lips. For a second, his mouth was warm and full on hers. Then she felt his lips brush the corner of her mouth and feather kisses along her jaw. They left a trail of fire and ice. When his mouth finally returned to hers, she held her breath. Still he didn't deepen the kiss. The pressure of his lips was so light. This wasn't the kind of kiss she'd expected from Roarke Farrell. Was that why it pulled at her so? Was that why she wasn't pushing him away? When she felt the scrape of his teeth on her bottom lip, she exhaled a ragged breath and her fingers slipped from the drawer handle. There was pleasure, sharp and sweet as his tongue moved over hers. She wasn't even aware when her hands moved to frame his face. She could feel the hard line of his cheekbone, then the silky softness of his hair, and finally the heat of his body when she pressed herself against it and deepened the kiss.

Roarke could have sworn that the kitchen floor shifted beneath his feet. He'd planned to be gentle with her. Her hands moving down his back erased the thought from his mind. He could taste the tangy flavor of wine on her tongue and warm honey in the deeper recesses of her mouth. His hunger grew. He'd expected resistance or submission. But her hands and mouth were urgent, demanding.

Too fast, C.J. thought while she still could. But instead of heeding the warning, her body tried to melt into his. She felt the pressure of each of his fingers as they moved through her hair. His mouth was no longer gentle on hers. It was hard and hot. She answered its demands. Wanting changed to needing in the length of time it took her to curl her fingers into his shirt. Then the need doubled in the time it took him to shift the angle of the kiss.

The slamming of the front door took several seconds to register in their minds. Paul's voice penetrated much more quickly.

"Roarke!"

At the sound of his name, Roarke stepped back, then steadied himself at the sink. He felt the immediate chill that the sudden separation created.

"Charlie!"

C.J. leaned against the counter and concentrated on breathing. Her body still tingled wherever it had been in contact with his. She let out a long breath . . . of relief or regret? She wasn't sure.

"Here you are." Paul breezed into the kitchen. For a moment he beamed at them both. Then he walked around the counter to envelop C.J. in a hug. With his arm still draped across her shoulders, he turned to Roarke. "I see you two are getting to know each other. What do you think of my daughter?"

C.J. glared at her father while Roarke found his voice.

"Daughter?" He stared at the two of them as the light began to dawn. Paul had often bragged about his kid. He had just assumed that "Charlie" was a son. Just as he had assumed . . . Slowly he relaxed against the sink to watch the little drama unfolding before him.

"You promised." C.J. bit out the words. "We agreed when I came here that no one would know I was your daughter."

"Roarke knows about you. He and I go way back. I told him about my kid, the lawyer."

She glared at Roarke. "You knew."

He shook his head. "About Charlie, yes. And Paul told me when he graduated from law school that he'd been offered a job in a prestigious Chicago firm." He paused thoughtfully. "And that he'd decided to take a job in the D.A.'s office instead. I assumed Charlie was his son." He smiled then. "If the *C* stands for 'Charlie,' what does the *J* stand for?"

"You—" she poked a finger into his chest "—are going to forget you ever heard that name. And as for you . . ." She whirled on her father. "He didn't know. Now, you've spoiled everything."

"He won't tell anyone. You can trust him."

"As far as I can spit," C.J. said.

"I won't tell a soul. Although I can't imagine why it's such a big secret. It certainly explains a lot."

"Right. It explains why Paul O'Shaughnessy took on an associate after all these years, doesn't it?" She began to pace. "He's got a kid who can't make it on her own. So he's taken the poor thing under his wing." She turned to glare at the two of them. "Well, I'm nobody's charity case! I intend to establish my reputation on my own. I will not build up a practice in criminal law by using my father's name."

Roarke might have smiled if he hadn't fine-tuned his instinct for survival, and if he hadn't sympathized with her situation. "I promise. I won't tell a soul."

After a moment, she nodded. "Thank you."

"What are friends for?"

She shot him a dark look before she walked away. "I'm going to start the fire for the steaks."

The two men watched her leave. Roarke shook his head slowly. "I should have guessed. She's inherited your temper."

Paul gave the younger man a shrewd glance. "You said the fact she's my daughter explained a lot. What?"

Roarke moved to the counter and picked up the ribbon of pasta. "Why you took on a young associate after all these years."

"And why exactly did you think I did that?"

Roarke met Paul's eyes. "I jumped to another conclusion."

"What? You didn't think . . ." Paul grinned. "I'll be damned. I feel ten years younger. At least." Then he frowned. "Is that what everyone assumed?" Without waiting for an answer, he began to pace. "She's used her mother's maiden name for years. It was more convenient after the divorce." He waved a hand. "She won't hear of changing it now. Wants to establish her career on her own." He stopped and turned to Roarke. "But I won't have people thinking that . . . that . . ."

"That you're having a little fling?" Roarke offered helpfully. It wasn't often that he had the pleasure of seeing Paul O'Shaughnessy squirm. It almost made up for all the sleep he'd lost since he'd met C.J. Finally he relented. "Relax. I don't think it's gone beyond vague speculation." He fed dough into the rollers. "Why didn't you ever mention that she was here?"

Paul pulled a glass out of the cupboard and poured wine into it. "I don't expect her to stay. She came after my surgery because she felt sorry for me. Now that I'm fully recovered, she'll leave. Her grandfather can offer her so much more. She could become a judge like her mother did." He lifted his glass to Roarke before taking a swallow. "There's only one person I've ever thought of working with, and the offer's still open. You're never going to be happy with the political side of the District Attorney's job. Besides, you belong in a courtroom, not pushing papers."

"Thanks for the offer, but you know why I won't accept. And you're wrong about C.J. She wants to be your partner."

"I'm depending on you to convince her of the wisdom of returning to Chicago."

Roarke nearly dropped a flat ribbon of dough. "No way. I'm not fond of banging my head against a brick wall."

Paul's crack of laughter filled the room. "All you have to do is make sure she loses the Williams case. I'm sure I can depend on you for that."

Roarke scowled as Paul continued, "I can still remember what it's like to lose a case when you believe that your client is innocent. It can make drawing up wills very attractive."

They were two of a kind, C.J. thought as she watched them from the doorway. And they were in for a surprise if they thought they could get rid of her that easily. "The fire's ready," she announced.

It gave her great pleasure to see them both start guiltily and then make themselves suddenly very busy laying out strips of pasta to dry. She hid a smile on the way to the refrigerator.

IT WAS DARK OUT when C.J. pulled her car into the parking lot of Patsy's Pub. Slowly she uncurled her fingers from the steering wheel. Then, with a sigh, she leaned her head against the seat. Dinner had been less than relaxing. How could she relax around Roarke Farrell after that kiss? Just thinking about it was enough to bring some of the feelings back.

She lifted her shoulders and dropped them. The back door of Patsy's Pub was open, and she could hear the band as well as laughter from the kitchen.

Just what was she going to do about Roarke Farrell? There was no use denying that he was a problem. He could make her bones melt and her brain turn to mush. And he could make her body act as if it belonged to someone else. The last thing she wanted or needed was to become involved with a lawyer, especially a prosecutor. Hadn't she learned anything in Chicago? Or from her parents? They had barely managed to live together until she was four. Two strong-willed people, each determined to have his or her own way. Until her mother had given up and gone back home to live with her parents.

For a second she rested her head against the steering wheel. No, she wasn't being fair. She would probably never know all the reasons why her mother had chosen to leave her father and take a position in her grandfather's law firm. Neither of her parents had ever fully explained it to her. She'd only been fourteen when her mother had died. And she'd never been able to ask her father. All she knew for sure was that her mother had never been happy because, even after the divorce, she'd never stopped loving her husband.

C.J. climbed out of her car and slammed the door. The solution was not to get involved. She had her rules. She'd stick to them. And she would be very careful to avoid any situation where Roarke would have the opportunity to kiss her again.

The locked door told her that the gallery had closed. The foyer was dim, lit only by the glow from the streetlight outside. Still, her eyes were immediately drawn to the white envelope lying on the floor. Stooping to pick it up, she saw that the letters of her name had been cut out of a newspaper and pasted on the front.

With a hurried glance over her shoulder, she pushed the door shut. Holding only the edge of the envelope, she carefully pulled the paper out.

"Drop the Williams case, or else."

Short and sweet, she thought as she felt a chill at the base of her spine. Someone knew where she lived. She reached out and rested her hand against the glass panel of the door, recalling Roarke's words. *A nitwit could break in.* Her glance dropped to the mail slot. But no one had. They probably hadn't even been in the building. The music and noise from Patsy's offered some comfort. At least she wasn't alone. Not yet. She looked through the glass to the deserted street. Still, if someone was watching, they would know when Patsy's closed for the night.

She carefully slipped the note back into the envelope. They wanted to scare her. She couldn't let them succeed. There was nothing to be gained by overreacting. It was just one anonymous note. Hadn't Roarke said he had a drawerful? The thought brought a smile to her face as she walked up the stairs to her apartment.

5

"COFFEE, COFFEE." C.J. whispered the word like a prayer as she groped her way to the kitchen. The sunshine pouring through the windows made her moan. She managed to get one eye open to push the Start button on the coffeemaker. Then she staggered back to the bedroom.

Monday mornings never seemed to get any better. With a steely resolve born of experience, she gave the bed a wide berth and crossed directly to her dresser. She snatched shorts from one drawer, a T-shirt and socks from another, then dragged them on. The shoes she carried with her to the kitchen, where she could breathe in the aroma of freshly brewing coffee.

By the time she'd had three sips from her mug and had finished her stretching exercises, C.J. was able to keep her eyes open without focusing all of her energy on it. She tied a sweatshirt around her waist and hurried out of her apartment before she was awake enough to talk herself out of it.

The sight of Roarke Farrell standing on the curb in the bright sunlight brought a pleasure so sharp and sweet that she couldn't recall one word of the cool little speech she had been rehearsing all weekend. Why did he have to look so great in running shorts? She was staring at the well-defined muscles in his legs when the dog beside him finally registered on her brain.

A German shepherd, she guessed, taking an involuntary step forward. He stood up as she approached.

"Hello, my beauty," she said softly as she sank to her knees and stretched out a hand so that the dog could smell her. As soon as the cold nose at her wrist was replaced by a rough tongue, she began to stroke his glossy coat with her other hand.

Roarke watched her in silence as she knelt at his feet caressing the dog. Her T-shirt fit snugly across her shoulders and upper arms. He could recall their slenderness and strength beneath his hands. Just as he could remember her scent and her taste. Not calling her over the weekend had been a part of his strategy. The effort that it had taken not to pick up the phone hadn't been. He wanted her. He'd discovered that much when he'd kissed her Friday evening, and her response told him that she wanted him, too. Finding out that Paul was her father should have simplified things. But it hadn't.

C.J. looked up at him and smiled. "I think I'm falling in love. What's his name?"

"McBride." He tried to ignore the warmth that began to spread through him. Love? Was that what he wanted from her?

"How long have you had him?"

"Since last night."

"I envy you," she said as she gave the dog a final pat and stood. "If I didn't live in the city, I'd love to have a dog."

"He's yours." Roarke handed her the leash.

"You're kidding."

"No."

"But . . . I can't accept him." She held out the leash, but Roarke had folded his arms across his chest.

"What's the problem? You just admitted that it was love at first sight. From what I can see the feeling is mutual."

C.J. dropped the hand that was still holding the leash to her side and began to pace back and forth on the sidewalk. McBride followed happily at her side. "It's impossible. An apartment is no place for a dog like this."

"He's used to living in the city. Besides, you could take him for a run every day and a walk in the evening."

She turned to face him. "How do you know what he's used to if you've only had him one night?"

"A friend of my mother's trained him."

C.J. looked at McBride. "I can't take him to work."

"Where there's a will, there's a way, Charlie."

Her head snapped up. "My name is not Charlie."

"What does the C stand for then?"

"It stands for itself. And stop trying to distract me. I can't keep this dog."

Roarke glanced at the building. "It seems to me that you have an ideal setup here. Sid and Doug have to open the restaurant for lunch. Why couldn't McBride spend most of the day in that courtyard behind the kitchen?"

She tapped her foot and frowned at him. "You think you have it all figured out."

"I aim to please."

Her gaze moved from Roarke to the dog. McBride looked up at her and wagged his tail. "You don't fight fair."

"No, I fight to win."

She met his eyes and responded instinctively to the challenge she saw there. "So do I."

Neither of them spoke for a moment. Then Roarke smiled. "How about a compromise? You could try him out."

"What do you mean?"

"Take him along on your run. My mother's friend raises and trains dogs specifically to make running safer for women."

C.J. gave him a dark look. "I should have known. Don't you ever give your protective instincts a rest?"

"Not when I know I'm right. And before you fly off the handle, you've got to admit McBride is better than a lecture."

The dog chose that moment to nuzzle her wrist. She glanced down at him and began to scratch behind his ears. "I can't argue with that."

"Then you'll give him a chance?"

C.J. looked into McBride's huge brown eyes. How could she refuse? "Oh, why not?"

When she began to jog up the hill away from her apartment, Roarke fell into step beside her. "Mind if I join you?"

"Do you want the truth?"

He laughed. "Question withdrawn. How's your training for the Charity Run coming along?"

"If you're smart, you'll withdraw that question, too."

"You haven't found anyone to take your place yet?"

"I will if it kills me. Either way, I'll probably end up dead. The hills on this course are murder." They crested the first one, and C.J. concentrated on catching her breath.

For a few blocks they ran in silence, broken only by the sound of running shoes slapping against pavement. The sun, still low in the sky, sent long shadows slanting across their path. As they passed an alley, C.J. caught the scent of stale beer and the more pungent odor of garbage.

When they heard the engine of an approaching car, Roarke dropped back, and McBride moved forward, giving it room to pass.

"He's well trained," C.J. said.

"I'll pass your approval along."

"That doesn't mean that I've decided to keep him."

"Heavens no."

As the pavement began to climb again to the college, C.J. turned her full attention to the run. There was no way she was going to falter in front of Roarke Farrell. When they finally reached the campus, she was panting.

"Want to rest for a minute?" Roarke asked.

"No way," she said. "I want to get back to my place so that I can murder Sid and Doug the moment I see them."

Once more they shifted into single file as a car passed them from behind. If it hadn't been for McBride's low growl, C.J. might not have noticed that it was the same blue station wagon that had driven by earlier.

"That car passed us before," Roarke said.

"It's probably some kids trying to find the right frat house." Even as she spoke, the car turned into the driveway of one of the large homes on the street.

At the next intersection, they turned and started their descent into the city. For the first time, C.J. relaxed.

At the foot of the hill, they turned down a street that led past Monroe High and into the business district. To the left and right of them, low-income apartment buildings alternated with old town houses and multiple-family houses that had seen better days.

"Tony Williams lives along here," C.J. said.

"So did I."

Nothing he could have said would have astonished her more. "You lived in this neighborhood?"

"I used to deliver newspapers along this very street. And I almost graduated from Monroe High. We moved away that year. That's when my uncle died and left my father his bar."

The conversation halted when C.J. ran ahead to make room for a bus to pass them. It lumbered to a stop at the end of the block, and she veered to the opposite side of the street to avoid the group of downtown workers pouring out of it. It was only when McBride growled that she noticed the blue station wagon pull slowly through the intersection. C.J. counted two people in the car. Sprinting across the street, she made a mental note of the license plate. Then she shook her head in annoyance. There was no doubt about it. The anonymous notes were making her paranoid.

Jogging in place, she turned back to check on Roarke. To her relief, he had stopped to tie his shoe. The last thing she needed was for him to become alarmed. So far, he'd given her a lecture and a dog. She wasn't sure she wanted to find out what he'd do if he thought she was really in danger. Not that she was. It was only her nerves that had her wondering about a blue station wagon.

She continued down the street, slowing her pace until Roarke caught up. She glanced at him then, intending to ask about his father's bar. One look dried her throat and erased the thread of their conversation from her mind. He had removed his T-shirt, and his skin glistened all over as though it had been massaged with oil. With no effort at all, she could imagine the way it would feel, smooth and slick, beneath her hands. And warm. An answering heat built in her own body. This close, she could see that he didn't have an ounce of fat anywhere. But she already knew that. She could remember quite clearly what it had felt like to be pressed hard against that body. The fit had been perfect. Giving her head a shake, she forced her eyes back to the road. How would she ever explain it if she tripped and fell at his feet?

They ran in silence until they turned the corner that would take them back to Patsy's. Then McBride seemed to sense that they were heading home and increased his pace. Laughing and breathless, she allowed the dog to pull her past the recessed doorway of her apartment, and it wasn't until she turned back that she noticed the little boy. She immediately pulled McBride to her side.

"Are you looking for someone?" Roarke asked.

The boy turned slowly and gave each of them a serious look. C.J. guessed his age to be about ten. He carried a small brown notebook and a cloth bag with several newspapers in it. "I'm waiting for C. J. Parker. He's never home when I come by to collect after school. I'm staying until he comes out."

"He's already out. I mean I am." Still winded from the run, she stopped to catch her breath. "I'm C. J. Parker. You must be my paper boy."

"Yes, sir . . . I mean ma'am." He glanced at his notebook. "You owe me $25.15."

"I'm sorry, Mr. . . ."

"Simmons."

C.J. held out her hand. The boy shook it. "Mr. Simmons, I didn't know you had taken over this route. Jimmie West used to collect on Sunday nights."

"I can't," he explained, but his eyes were on McBride.

"Yes, well, why don't you hold my dog for me while I run upstairs to get your money?" She held out the leash to him and had the satisfaction of seeing him smile for the first time.

When she returned, the boy was deep in conversation with Roarke about the profit margins of paper routes. She listened long enough to learn that paper boys made most of their money from tips and thanked her stars that she had included a generous one in the check she had written. As soon as the boy turned to her, she handed it to him. "I've written it for what I owe plus a month in advance. Why don't you leave me an envelope in May with your address on it and I could mail it to you after that."

"Oh, sure," the boy said with a smile. "Mr. Farrell says that you might be interested in having someone walk McBride in the afternoons. I could do it after I finish school."

"I told him that he could stop in at Patsy's and one of the owners would fetch the dog," Roarke added.

"You think of everything, don't you, Mr. Farrell?"

"Just trying to be of help."

Turning so that the boy was behind her, she whispered, "In a pig's eye."

"It does solve one of your problems," Roarke pointed out.

C.J. opened her mouth, then shut it. She was looking at her biggest problem. Where was she going to find a solution for him? She dropped her gaze to the dog. McBride was minor in comparison. She turned back to the boy, and managed a smile when she shook his hand. "My phone number's on the check. Give me a call tomorrow."

The moment the boy was out of sight, C.J. turned on Roarke. "You can wipe that grin off your face. I'm going to keep McBride for two weeks. If it doesn't work out, you'll take him back and find a good home for him."

"Sounds fair."

C.J. frowned. "Well, it's not. It's not fair at all."

"Why not?"

"I wish I didn't like you."

He was totally unprepared for the feeling that ran through him. Unnerved, he didn't even know he had taken a step toward her until she raised her hand and stepped back. "No, let me finish. I don't want to like you. But you bring me a dog. You're even nice to small boys. It's got to stop."

"Okay, I won't bring you another dog. How about a cat?"

C.J. fought the impulse to smile. "Don't try to get me off on a tangent. I want to finish this."

"Go ahead." Roarke enjoyed watching her as she marshaled her thoughts. Damp from the run, her hair had darkened, the gold losing out to the red. He caught a curl and rubbed it between his thumb and finger. It felt cool. Odd when its color promised fire.

C.J. knocked his hand away. "Pay attention. I like you, but that's as far as it's going to go. We are not going to date, and we're not going to become involved, except professionally. Is that clear?"

"Not quite. Since the liking is mutual, maybe you won't mind explaining why we're not going to become involved?"

"We're both lawyers."

"Maybe one of us could change careers."

"I'm serious."

"I can see that. But I'm afraid I'm a little dense. What's wrong with our both being lawyers?"

C.J. began to pace back and forth on the pavement. McBride followed at her side. "We're adversaries on the Williams case. There could be a conflict of interest."

"The trial will be over eventually," Roarke pointed out as his gaze dropped to her legs. The shorts she wore afforded him a full view of their slim, shapely length.

C.J. waved a hand and continued to pace. "We'll always be antagonists. We work on opposite sides of the criminal justice system. Plus there's the fact that we're both competitive. We both like to win. One of us is going to lose."

"Anything else?" Roarke put some effort into shifting his gaze back to her face. If he was going to make any kind of a case for himself, he had to concentrate on her argument.

"We're at different phases in our careers. I'm starting out. You're about to achieve your goal. You'll be the new District Attorney in the fall. We're totally out of sync."

"On the one hand we're too much alike, but on the other hand we're too different?"

"Yes." C.J. turned to look at him then. Arms crossed, he was leaning against the wall. Yet he wasn't relaxed. She could sense the tension in his body almost as clearly as she felt it in her own.

"And the bottom line is that I'm the last person in the world you want to get involved with?"

For just a second, C.J. hesitated. It sounded so blunt, but it was exactly what she had thought to herself countless times. "Yes."

"Obviously you've given this a great deal of thought."

His voice sounded so reasonable. She didn't trust it for a minute. "Yes, I have."

"What kind of man are you looking for?"

"I'm not. At least not right now. Maybe later, after I get my practice established."

"And then?" Roarke pressed on. "What will he be like?"

"Different." C.J. found it took a great deal of effort to conjure up an image of her ideal man with a half-naked Roarke Farrell standing only a few feet away. "More laid back than I am. Someone I can relax with . . . someone I can talk to without arguing about a case."

"Someone to play Parcheesi with?" Roarke prompted helpfully.

C.J. blinked. She'd never played Parcheesi in her life. It made her think of front porches and rocking chairs. "I guess."

"What would the two of you talk about?"

She racked her brain frantically. Not Parcheesi. Not lawsuits. "Shakespeare," she finally said in desperation.

"And sports?" Roarke suggested. "The weather per- haps?"

C.J. nodded and wondered how she and her ideal man had ended up in rockers discussing the weather.

"You're going to get plenty of sleep with this guy. He'll bore you to death. And in the meantime I'm off-limits?"

"Correct."

"Good."

She had forgotten how quickly he could move. Be- fore she could even sense his intention, he had closed the distance between them and his hands gripped her shoulders. The kiss was hard and potent, giving her body a will of its own. Her lips parted eagerly beneath his, her arms circled his waist. He smelled of sunshine, tasted of salt and heat. His skin felt cool and slick un- der her hands. Even as it started to heat, he pulled away. She wasn't sure how she managed to remain standing.

"I'm glad we had this little conversation," he said. "Just remember, Counselor, forbidden fruit is always irresistible."

She slumped against the building as she watched him jog easily away. How could his legs work? Hers felt like jelly. It was only when McBride began to lick her wrist that she looked down and realized she had dropped his leash.

"Damn! And double damn!" She cursed Roarke Far- rell fluently all the way up the stairs to her apartment.

"SORRY I'M LATE," C.J. said as she hurried into Paul's office with McBride in tow.

He grunted a greeting and gestured toward a steam- ing mug of coffee at the edge of his desk.

C.J. grabbed it and took a grateful sip. There'd been no time to drink any at home. Settling herself into a chair, she draped McBride's leash over the arm. The dog sank to the floor with a sigh that drew Paul's immediate attention.

"What in hell is that? A new client?" he asked.

"No, he's a . . . a friend."

"Good thinking. I sure as hell wouldn't want him as my enemy."

"His name's McBride, and I haven't been able to make any arrangements for him yet." She reached into her briefcase, pulled out the report on Jarvis Johnson and placed it on Paul's desk. "If you have a minute I'd like you to look over what Sam Hillerman dug up on Tony's friend Jarvis Johnson."

Paul opened the manila folder. "You're trying to make me forget that there's a dog in my law office."

"Just for today," she assured him and relaxed as soon as he began to skim through the file. After a few moments, Paul let out a low whistle. "Three prior arrests for assault. Why in hell didn't they book him that night instead of your client?"

"Everyone saw Tony holding the bat."

Paul leaned back in his chair and pursed his lips.

"Jarvis hasn't been in trouble since he turned sixteen. He's either reformed or he's being careful," C.J. said.

"Careful enough to make sure that someone else was holding the bat? Maybe your client's covering for Johnson."

"I'm seeing him later today, and I'll ask him. Not that it will do much good if he's telling the truth about the amnesia. The person I have to talk to is Jarvis."

"No!" McBride let out a soft bark. Even C.J. was startled by the vehemence in her father's voice. Paul rose and began to pace behind his desk. "I have a bad feeling about this whole thing. Especially about this Johnson boy."

The dog had risen with Paul. C.J. patted McBride's head before she replied. "He's only a kid."

"He's old enough to know how to manipulate the system."

"I'm not going to do anything foolish. And besides, I have McBride here to protect me."

Paul scowled at the dog.

C.J. continued. "We've been through this before. I'm going to practice criminal law. Here or on my own."

"I have your word that you'll take the dog with you?"

C.J. smiled. "I brought him here, didn't I?"

"Hmmph." Paul sat down, but he was still frowning.

"Have you had any luck yet in locating a witness who can back up Sandra Hughes's story?"

Paul swiveled in his chair to study the map he had fastened to the wall behind his desk. It was an enlargement of the streets surrounding the Farberville residence of Alexander Day, the millionaire businessman Sandra was accused of shooting. C.J. knew that her father hired Sam Hillerman to find someone, anyone who could corroborate his client's story that she'd seen a large black car pull out of the Days's driveway just before she'd turned into it on the morning of the murder. "Sam has interviewed people in every house in that neighborhood. No one saw a thing. They didn't even see Sandra arrive. These people are so damn rich, they live way back off the road behind fences or walls. At eight forty-five in the morning the shuttle Atlantis could land on that street and no one would notice it."

C.J. rose and walked to the wall to study the map more closely. "Any school bus stops nearby?"

"The last pickup is eight o'clock. The husbands leave for work by eight-thirty. Sandra claims she saw the car pull out at a quarter of nine."

"How about hired help?"

"What do you mean?"

"Maids, gardeners, carpet cleaners, repairmen? Rich people hire other people to work for them. The ones that Grandma hired usually came after we'd cleared out of the house for the day."

Paul stared thoughtfully at the map for a moment. "You may have something there."

He was reaching for the phone when McBride scrambled to his feet with a bark. C.J. unhooked the leash from the arm of the chair, and the dog pulled her to the door that led from Paul's office to hers.

"Are you expecting anyone this early?" asked Paul.

"No." Opening the door, C.J. peered into an empty room.

"Ruth?" Paul walked past her. The door to the reception area stood wide open. He poked his head through it. "That's funny." Then he shrugged. "Maybe it was someone passing by in the hall." On his way back to his own office, he stopped to pat McBride on the head. "Keep up the good work, boy. You take good care of her."

It wasn't until C.J. closed the door to the reception area that she remembered. It hadn't been open when she'd arrived. She had been late for her meeting with Paul, and she'd gone directly to his office without passing through her own. A quick glance around the room reassured her that nothing had been disturbed. Then she saw the envelope on her desk. It was propped up against the vase of flowers. She crossed slowly toward it. It was blank and unsealed, the flap merely tucked in. She picked it up and held her breath as she pulled out the single page and unfolded it.

"Drop the Williams case or else."

A shiver of fear raced down her spine. The letters had been cut out of newspaper headlines. The ones forming "or else" were larger, more sinister looking than the one she'd found in the foyer. Someone was taking time preparing these messages. And going to a lot of trouble to deliver them. C.J. glanced over her shoulder at the closed door. Had someone followed her to work? When she tried to swallow and found her throat was dry, a tiny flame of anger began to replace the fear.

She started to pace back and forth and immediately tangled herself in McBride's leash. She dropped it, stepped free and crossed the room to sit behind her desk. No way was she going to allow anonymous notes to frighten her. The dog roamed around the room, then chose to settle near her chair. Recalling the way he'd barked at the noise in her office, she smiled. Hopefully she wasn't the only one with a dry throat this morning. She slid the letter back into the envelope carefully, and placed it in her top drawer. The other one was safe in her desk at home along with the license plate number she'd jotted down after her run with Roarke. Once again she thought of Roarke's collection of hate mail. She was smiling as she drew Tony's file out of her briefcase.

AN HOUR LATER, C.J. placed two piles of little colored dots on the map of Sutton Street that she had spread across the top of her desk. Then she glanced at her watch. Tony was due any minute, and she could feel the tension already beginning to build in her shoulders. Her relationship with her new client was still uneasy, at best.

She breathed deeply, concentrated on tightening every muscle in her body and then suddenly let them go limp. It was an exercise her mother had taught her. They'd often practiced it together before going downstairs to dine with her grandparents.

At the buzzing of the intercom, McBride raised his head and growled.

"Easy," she said as she crossed to the patch of sunlight that he'd chosen to sprawl in for his nap. "This is a friend." Then she moved to the door and opened it. "Tony," she said in greeting as the boy walked past her and slumped into the chair farthest from her desk.

Tony picked up a magazine from a nearby table, rolled it into a tight tube and tapped it against his knee. Clearly he was not happy to be here. Still he'd come. She had to concentrate on the positive.

When McBride whined a greeting, Tony dropped the magazine and turned to stare at the dog. "Yours?" he asked.

"Yes."

McBride rose and walked over to sniff Tony's hand. Then, satisfied, he gave it a lick. Tony began to scratch behind the dog's ears.

After watching for a minute, C.J. walked behind her desk and sat down in her chair. "I want you to tell me again what happened that night."

Tony continued to scratch the dog. "I already did."

She picked up her pen and opened her notebook. "This time I want you to show me. On this map."

He looked at it, then at her. "You've got my statement. I don't remember anything else."

For a brief moment as she met his eyes steadily, she saw a flash of pain and frustration before the shutter dropped into place. If sympathy would have helped, she would have given it. Instead she laid down her pen and shrugged. "Your mother is paying for my time. If you want to waste it . . ."

Tony dropped his hand from the dog's head, rose and dragged the chair closer. McBride followed and propped his chin on the desk.

C.J. pointed to the colored pieces of paper. "The orange dots are Danny and his friends. The blue dots are Jarvis and Larry and you. Start from where you all met on Sutton Street and move them along as you tell me what happened."

She waited, watching as he placed them all at the corner of the street. "Where did you park your car?"

Tony pointed to a spot in the middle of the block.

"Start there then. Did Jarvis drive?"

"No. He rode shotgun. Larry was in the back seat."

C.J. began to jot down notes as the boy moved the blue dots one by one to join the orange dots. Just as she'd hoped, the map was proving to be a distraction. Already Tony was adding new details to the story he had committed to memory after countless repetitions. When he was fully caught up in it, she'd ask about his relationship with Jarvis Johnson. She could only hope and pray that she would learn something new. Anything.

HOURS LATER, C.J. barely heard the knock on her door. Paul was halfway across the room before she glanced up.

"What's all this?" He pointed to the circles of colored paper that dotted the map spread across her desk.

C.J. rubbed the back of her neck. "The orange ones are the college kids. The blue ones are Tony and his friends. I've been reading through the statements and moving them around."

"Any luck?"

"Not yet." She indicated the two piles of paper next to her. "I've only made it through the first stack."

"I can't talk you into an early dinner?"

"I promised myself I'd stay here until I finished them."

"How'd your meeting with Tony go?"

C.J. shrugged. "He knew about Jarvis's arrests, but he claims he wouldn't lie to protect him."

"You believe him?"

"I believe his amnesia's genuine."

Paul sat on the edge of the desk. "I have a suggestion."

C.J. stared at her father. He had a lot of suggestions. But he seldom felt the need to preface them with an announcement.

"Why don't you visit Monroe High tomorrow and interview one of those..." He paused to run a hand through his hair. "I'm not sure what they call them nowadays."

"Teachers?" C.J. asked.

"Very funny. We used to call them advisors... or something like that."

"Guidance counselors," she guessed.

"Whatever. One of them might be able to give you a line on the Johnson boy—and on Tony for that matter."

C.J. regarded him levelly. "How long did it take you to hatch this little plot?"

"What do you mean?" His eyes had taken on the bland, innocent look she had learned to distrust.

"The plot to send me to Jarvis's school. With any luck at all, I might get to interview him right in the principal's office with plenty of people around to protect me."

Paul shrugged. "It's a good idea."

"I agree." She smiled and turned her appointment book around so he could read it. "I have an appointment to see Mrs. Kingsley, Jarvis's guidance counselor, tomorrow morning."

"When did you decide to do this?"

"While I was talking with Tony."

He frowned. "I didn't think of it until a few moments ago."

"Jealous?"

"Of course not."

"Maybe you could trust me not to do anything foolish."

"Maybe I'll leave while we're still pretty much in agreement." C.J. watched him saunter to the door. He was smiling when he turned to close it behind him.

MCBRIDE'S WHINE WOKE C.J. out of a sound sleep. The darkness outside startled her and she checked her watch. Eight o'clock. She couldn't have been asleep for long. She ran a hand through her hair as she placed the statement she'd been working on back in its pile. She rose and stretched, then froze when she heard the door to the outer office open and close. McBride whined once more, then moved around the desk.

For a moment there was silence. C.J. held her breath. The footsteps were barely audible. She couldn't hear them at all when the dog began to whine again. She slipped off her shoes and circled to the front of her desk. Her fingers closed around the vase sitting on the edge of the desk, and she carried it with her to the door. McBride was silent, but alert. She heard a floorboard creak as the footsteps came closer and closer. Slowly the doorknob turned. With the vase held high, she stepped to one side. The instant the door opened she swung her arms down.

6

THE VASE MISSED ROARKE by inches, but only because McBride's ecstatic greeting backed him up a step. Relief washed through C.J. as she stared at the splintered fragments of glass on the floor. If she'd hit him . . . Suddenly her knees gave out, and she slumped against the wall.

"You're never happy to see me but this is—" The moment Roarke saw her face, he grabbed her arm and dragged her to a chair. He helped her sit down and press her head between her legs, then signaled McBride to her side. "Stay," he ordered before he moved away.

C.J. watched a trickle of water wind its way across the floor to the wall. It might have been Roarke's blood. Nausea bubbled up in her stomach as she tried to push the image away.

"Drink this." Roarke pushed a glass into her hand.

She took a swallow and shivered as the liquid burned her throat.

"Again." He crouched at the side of her chair and watched her drain the glass. When she finally looked at him, he said, "That's a hell of a way to greet clients."

C.J. managed a smile. "McBride may have saved your life."

"We'll give him a medal." He took the glass and set it aside. When her gaze followed it, he cupped her chin in his hand so that she had to look at him. "What's going on here?"

"I heard a noise. It spooked me."

He shook his head. "Not good enough. The woman who flipped me at the track doesn't spook that easily." He laced his fingers with hers. "What happened?"

The warmth from his hand flowed into hers. She might have pulled away from that, but there was strength, too. For just a moment she allowed herself to hold on to it. "I've received two anonymous notes, one last Friday night and another this morning."

"Where are they?"

"One's at my apartment. The other's in the top drawer."

He rose and moved quickly to the desk. Holding the envelope by its corners, he examined it carefully. The lack of address worried him. "It didn't come in the mail."

"No. I found it on my desk this morning. Someone delivered it while I was meeting with Paul."

"He's seen it?"

"No. And I don't want him to."

Roarke reread the brief warning. And she'd still stayed late to work alone. His anger and frustration flared as he remembered how easily he'd gotten into her office. But he quickly pushed his emotions aside. They would only interfere with his ability to handle her. He put the note back in the drawer. "Any idea who sent it?"

She shook her head.

"How about your client?"

She stared at him then, and he had the satisfaction of seeing the last trace of fear disappear from her eyes. "My client? If he wants me off the case, all he has to do is fire me. And don't give me any of that crap about his trying to manipulate the system. What about your client?"

"What's his motive? I'm going to win this case for him."

"In your dreams." She rose from her chair. "What are you doing here anyway, sneaking around like a thief?"

"I came to check on McBride." It was a lie. He'd come to see her. All day long he'd been weighing his options. Avoiding her for a few days would have been a much better strategy, but he hadn't been able to stay away.

"Check on him all you want, but hurry it up. I'm going to clean up this mess and take him home."

Roarke watched in amusement as she sailed out of the room. C.J. in a temper was preferable to the white-faced, shaken woman of a few moments ago. When she returned with a broom and a dustpan, he leaned over to scratch McBride behind the ears.

"He seems in good spirits."

"He should be. He's done nothing but sleep all day." She sank to her knees and began to pick up the wilted flowers.

Roarke glanced around the room. It was small, sparsely furnished and neat. The reports she'd been working on were stacked evenly on her desk. The coffee cup sitting next to them was clean. The room reflected her. Everything in it seemed organized, efficient. It was the complete antithesis of his own cluttered work space.

"Nice place you have here."

She tossed more flowers and glass into the wastebasket.

The one painting on the wall contrasted with the monastic neatness of the room. It contained an explosion of red tulips. His gaze returned to C.J. The overhead light picked up the red glints in her hair.

"Damn!" C.J. dropped the piece of glass she was holding and tried to stop the flow of blood from her finger.

"Here, let me." Roarke was beside her in a second, examining the wound with a practiced eye. "I think...yes." He grasped her finger firmly and squeezed it. All C.J. could see was blood, but Roarke held up the tiny shard of glass he'd managed to remove. He squeezed her finger once more before he wrapped it tightly in his handkerchief. Then he pressed his mouth briefly against her knuckles just above the makeshift bandage.

C.J. felt her whole system jolt as her eyes locked with his. Tiny ribbons of heat unfurled up her arm, making her skin burn even as she suppressed a shiver. Any second she was going to tremble. When he moved his free hand to her cheek, she grasped his wrist. The speed of his pulse quickened her own. She could have withdrawn her hand, but she didn't.

Roarke could see everything she was thinking and feeling as her eyes darkened. He'd promised himself that he wouldn't touch her, not tonight. But his fingers brushed along her skin, moving to the back of her neck as if they had a will of their own. He shouldn't have come. He had only to look at her mouth to remember her taste. The memory alone had the need churning inside of him.

As he urged her closer, C.J.'s fingers tightened on his wrist. In protest or acceptance? She wasn't sure. The moment his mouth touched hers, she didn't care. The feelings, the longings she'd been pushing away for days erupted instantly and with such intensity that she could no longer deny them. Desire was a burning, melting sensation that raced through her, making her desperate. With one hand she clutched at his shirt. The other found its way to the back of his head to pull him closer. As his taste poured into her, she forgot everything, her plans, her goals. All she wanted was Roarke. Only Roarke.

In some corner of his mind, Roarke knew he wasn't being gentle as he combed his fingers through her hair, then shifted the angle of the kiss. In the honeyed recesses of her mouth he found the taste that he'd been craving. He dragged one hand down the length of her spine to close over her hip. Spreading his fingers, he pressed her closer. Softness against hardness. Suddenly, he felt as if he were drowning in her. He had to think. Control. Had he ever come this close to losing it? He broke off the kiss and rested his cheek against hers. He dragged in a breath, and her scent filled him. He felt weak when he finally pulled away.

The eyes she lifted to meet his were dazed. He waited, holding her until they slowly focused. The moment they did, she stiffened. "I can't . . . We can't."

"Can't what? Want each other? We do, and it's not going to go away."

She couldn't deny it, not when she was still weak from the feelings he'd unleashed in her. She lifted a hand to her hair and discovered that it had come loose. How? Had she been that lost? It was only as she pulled free of his hands that she realized she was still on her knees.

She wasn't sure she could stand. "We'll just have to deal with this."

Roarke tried to control the surge of temper that was swiftly displacing the passion he'd felt only seconds before. "Deal with it? I have a few suggestions."

"No." She was trembling. "I'm not ready."

It was the trace of fear in her eyes that stopped him. He'd never seen it there before, not even that morning at the track. His anger evaporated. "I'll agree to a postponement, Charlie. I'm not sure how long."

She managed a shaky smile. "I'll take what I can get."

McBride nuzzled his way between them and gave them each a slobbery kiss, easing the tension between them.

"I think he's hungry," C.J. said as she got to her feet.

"Sit down and put some pressure on that finger while I finish cleaning up this mess. I have dog food in the car."

C.J. GRIPPED HER KEY and pushed it into the lock. There was no way she was going to linger in the hallway, not with Roarke Farrell breathing down her back. She had planned to bid him a firm farewell in his car. But he was carrying his perfect excuse for seeing her to the door — a fifty-pound bag of dog food. There was no way she could have lugged that sucker up the stairs. Her only regret was that she didn't live in a ten-floor walk-up.

Her foot hit it the moment she stepped into the room. She heard the whispery sound as it slid across the hardwood floor. The only light in the room came from the streetlamps outside, but she could see the white envelope quite clearly. Still, she flipped the wall switch, hoping she was wrong. Then she walked quickly to pick it up. McBride moved away to explore the apartment, and behind her she heard Roarke unload his burden. With steely self-control she opened the envelope. When she turned, she was smiling.

"'Drop the Tony Williams case, or else.' Not very inventive, are they?" she asked as she dropped the note on the table in front of her couch. Then she slipped out of her shoes and walked to her stereo.

Roarke watched her as she sorted through several CDs before inserting one into her stereo. Over the years, he'd watched his mother cope with crises by following her regular routine. He decided to give C.J. some time before they talked.

The soothing sound of strings floated out into the room. When McBride drew her attention by rubbing against her leg, she responded immediately, unhooking his leash and scratching behind his ears. Finally she turned to Roarke again and smiled. "Would you like some white wine?"

"Sure." He waited until she disappeared through an archway to the left before he moved to the windows at the far end of the room and checked the locks. From the looks of it the note had been slipped under the door, but he wouldn't leave until he had made sure the apartment was secure.

The first of the two doors to his right led to a small bathroom, the second to a bedroom. While he methodically checked the windows, his mind recorded other details. The bed was antique brass, old and polished, with a white lace coverlet that matched the curtains. The only splash of color that drew the eye was the watermelon-colored chaise longue. He walked to it and ran his hand over the fabric. Its velvety texture reminded him of her skin. The candle on the nearby table smelled of vanilla. Next to it lay a leather-bound volume of the New York State penal code. With very little effort he could picture C.J. stretched out on the lounge in something flimsy preparing an argument for court. With even less effort he could imagine lying there beside her with those slender, strong legs wrapped around him. He drew in a deep breath to clear his head. Later, he promised himself as he hurried back to the living room and hoisted the dog food onto his shoulders. He passed C.J. in the archway to the kitchen.

"Just in time," she remarked. "He's staging a sit-down strike in front of his water dish." She set her tray down on the coffee table, picked up a glass and sipped. She allowed the cool, fruity flavor to linger on her tongue for a moment before she swallowed. Then she sat down and closed her eyes. Above the music, she could hear the rumble of Roarke's voice in the kitchen as he talked to McBride. If she concentrated hard enough, she could believe that it was just an ordinary day and that the note lying on the table in front of her was simply a prank.

By the time Roarke joined her, she'd almost convinced herself that it was true. Smiling, she handed him a glass. He carried it to the nearby bookshelves and studied the photographs. Most were snapshots of Paul, golfing or fishing. One, larger than the others, caught his attention. Two women sat stiffly posed on a sofa with a young girl between them. It took him a moment to recognize C.J. Her hair hung in long braids over her shoulders. There was a sadness in her expression that he hadn't seen before. Curious, he placed it on the coffee table when he took a seat next to her. "Special occasion?" he asked and watched her smile fade when she glanced at it.

"Mother's Day," she said.

"Not a happy one?" he asked quietly.

She took another swallow of wine. "My grandparents had it taken for some society column to commemorate three generations of Julia Parkers. The only problem was that I wasn't Julia the third. They never forgave my mother and Paul for putting his mother's name first.

"Charlie?" Roarke guessed.

"Short for Charlotte."

He grinned. "Charlotte Julia."

She regarded him coolly over her wineglass. "My legal name is C.J. After the divorce, my mother went through the process of changing our last names to Parker. While she was at it, she switched my first name, too, so that I wouldn't be named after anyone. It was one of the very few times she stood up to her family. The only other time was when she married my father. But that hardly counts since she left him."

"You're angry with her," Roarke said.

"No, I . . ." C.J. sighed. "Maybe, a little. For giving up too easily. She let men dominate her life. Oh, she'd put up a fight for a while. She stuck it out with my father until I was four. I can remember lying awake in bed and listening to them argue. But in the end she let him drive her away. Then she allowed my grandfather to treat her as a figurehead in his law firm. All he ever allowed her to work on was estates and trusts. And she wanted trial work." When she noticed that her fingers had tightened on her wineglass, she set it on the table.

"Paul mentioned that she was a judge."

"Thanks to my grandfather's political contributions. But she died in an auto accident before she ever sat on the bench."

"I'm sorry." Roarke took her hands in his. She might not want to admit the anger, but he could feel it.

"It was a long time ago."

Roarke glanced at the picture one last time. He wanted to know more about her family, but there were other things he had to deal with tonight. Lifting the note from the table, he said, "I think we ought to call the police."

"No!" The word came out more sharply than she had intended.

"Promise me that you'll at least talk to Paul about it."

"No. I don't want him to know. That's why I can't tell the police. It would get back to him."

"There's more to this than Paul's health." He reached for the wine bottle. "Why don't you tell me about it?"

For the length of time it took him to refill their glasses, she reviewed her options and decided to go with the truth. "My father doesn't want me to do criminal work. He didn't want my mother to do it, either. That's one of the reasons she left him." She sipped her wine. "If I run to him for help, he'll worry. Worse, he'll start to hover over me, and eventually he'll interfere. Promise me you won't tell him."

"All right. For the moment we won't tell Paul or the police. Who besides your father wants you off the case?"

C.J. gave him a long, level look. "The person who really hit Danny Jasper on the head."

"I thought about that, but it doesn't make sense. Why would the person who really hit Danny want you off the case. It would just mean another delay, and surely they'd want Tony convicted as quickly as possible."

C.J. clasped her hands together in her lap. "Unless it's my father they're worried about. It's no secret that I work in his office. Maybe they'd prefer to have a delay rather than run the risk of having Paul O'Shaughnessy anywhere near the case."

Roarke studied her for a moment. "It's possible. But it's also possible that if they succeed in scaring you off, Paul would take over the case. Tony or one of his friends might be hoping for that to happen."

C.J. met his eyes steadily. "No. My client wouldn't do something like that."

"That still leaves his friends."

"Or Danny Jasper's friends. Maybe they just want to scare me enough so that I can't do a good job."

Roarke took a drink of his wine and set his glass on the table. Then he laced his fingers behind his head and leaned back against the cushions. "Okay, for the sake of discussion, let's say you're right, and someone else hit Danny that night. Any idea who it might be?"

C.J. gaped at him. "You're willing to concede Tony might not be guilty?"

"Let's say I'm willing to brainstorm all the possibilities."

She opened her mouth to reply, then shut it. He looked so relaxed and sounded so innocent that for a moment she'd almost forgotten he was the enemy. "I won't discuss my theories on this case with you."

He grinned. "Fine. We'll discuss mine then. Suppose Tony's innocent, wittingly or unwittingly covering for one of his friends. This so-called friend wants a quick conviction and gets upset with the postponement and with the new attorney. He's motivated not so much by logic as by anger and fear."

It was altogether too close to one of her own ideas on the subject, but she managed to keep her expression blank. "I still say it could be one of Danny's friends."

"Nah. I could drive a truck through that premise. Why would Tony cover for one of them? And how did one of them get hold of Tony's bat?"

"Maybe he dropped it."

"Right. They pick it up, bash their friend's head in and very politely hand it back to Tony when they're finished with it. Besides, why would one of them hit Danny?"

"It could have been an accident."

Roarke shook his head. "Wishful thinking."

"Maybe they're all covering up something."

"Who's *they*? Tony's friends or Danny's friends? I can buy the fact that they'd each protect their own, but why would all of them turn against Tony?"

"This is ridiculous!" C.J. said.

"I agree. As a theory, it has a certain laughable quality."

She waved a hand. "That's not what I mean. What's ridiculous is that we're discussing the case, and we can't."

Roarke leaned forward and placed a hand on her arm. "That's where you're wrong, Counselor. We were talking about my ideas, and I feel perfectly comfortable sharing them with you. I haven't in any way jeopardized the state's case. And there are lots of things that you can talk about without giving away your defense. One of them is whether or not you get any more notes or phone calls. I'll be checking with you on a daily basis."

C.J. glared at him. "You're crazy if you think—"

"Your choice, Charlie. Me or the police."

She sat rigidly, trying to reel in her temper. "I have to prove that I can handle this by myself."

"To your father maybe. Not to me." Though he was only touching her arm, he could feel the anger simmering in her.

"You're just like him!" It was the wrong thing to say. She knew it the minute the words were out. Their faces were very close. She watched his eyes darken from smoke to almost black, and it was more than anger she saw in them.

"I'm not your father." Roarke thought of his plans for her, the ones that had called for patience, for slow, subtle seduction. They needed revision, he decided, as he pulled her close and covered her mouth with his.

She'd had time to prepare herself, she thought. And she'd known what to expect. She could feel his anger in the movement of his mouth on hers, but what she tasted was need. Her defenses began to slip away. One scrape of his teeth, one sweep of his hand and the response flowed out of her. It was as if no time at all had elapsed since the last time he'd kissed her.

If she'd been able to think, she might have been frightened. But her body was so attuned to his that all she could do was feel. She could taste the wine that still lingered on his tongue. She could feel the strength of his hands as they moved over her, pressing, molding. The cushions of the couch were impossibly soft at her back, his body incredibly hard as he crushed her into them. Her hands framed his face, then slipped into his hair.

She forgot her rules and all the reasons for them. She thought only of him as she pulled him closer.

Roarke wondered if he would ever get used to her response. Or was it his own that had him reeling? He dragged his mouth from hers and rained kisses over her face. Her scent grew stronger at her temple, more elusive at her throat, more exotic beneath her ear. He breathed deeply and wanted more. Hard and hot, his lips returned to hers. Desperate, his tongue probed deeper. He discovered the familiar flavor, sweet, hot, ripe. When he pulled her blouse free and found the smooth silk of her skin, he suddenly wanted much more than he'd intended to take when he'd pulled her into his arms.

Closer. The word pounded in her blood as his hands were moving over her. Burning her breast, bruising her waist, they explored her with a thoroughness that brought all her wants and needs shooting to the surface. When his fingers slid beneath her skirt to stroke the inside of her thigh she tightened her grip on his shoulders and whispered his name like a plea.

From a great distance, a phone began to ring. He could barely hear it above the beating of his heart. Even when the shrill sound finally penetrated, he barely found the strength to draw away. The answering machine kicked in.

"I'm not home at the present time. Please leave a message after the tone."

At the sound of her own voice, C.J. felt the mists begin to clear. Roarke was still close. Too close? Not close enough? She watched his hand reach for a glass of wine. It wasn't steady. She took comfort in that. Then the whisper hissed out into the room.

"We know where you work, where you live, where you run. Drop the Williams case before it's too late!"

Her skin, burning only moments before, turned cold. But even as it did, anger brought her up off the couch. Roarke beat her to the phone and picked it up, tilting the receiver so that she could hear the dial tone.

"Two notes and a phone call in one day. They're trying very hard to scare you off the case."

He saw no fear in her eyes when she said, "It won't work."

"Yeah." He was angry but he couldn't allow it to interfere with what he had to do. "That's what has me worried. What do you think they'll do when they finally figure that out?"

C.J.'s face paled, but she answered calmly, "I can handle it by myself."

"If you were a man, you wouldn't have to. You could go to Paul." He held the receiver out to her. "As it is, you have a choice. Call the police or settle for me."

She felt trapped. "I meant what I said this morning. I want to keep our relationship strictly professional."

"Fine." He cradled the receiver and moved to the couch.

"Fine?" She followed at his heels. "We're on opposite sides of this case, and you want to become my... my confidant!"

He turned to her. "I want to become your lover. At the moment I'll settle for being your friend."

She opened her mouth, shut it and stared. Her lover. She would not allow herself to think about what might have happened if the phone hadn't rung. His hair was still mussed by her hands. The top two buttons of his shirt had pulled open. He looked as though he had just stepped out of a whirlwind or off a roller coaster. He looked exactly the way she felt. And he was calmly talking about being her friend. "That's impossible!" she said and wished with all her heart that it wasn't.

"Nonsense." He sat down on the couch and forced himself to relax. "Your father and I have been adversaries for years. We've also been friends."

C.J. wanted to pace. She wanted to pound on the walls. Instead she sat down in the chair across from him. "I have to put my client first."

"Yes. And he deserves one-hundred percent of your attention. How can you expect to give him that when you'll be spending half your time looking over your shoulder?"

He was right. She could damn him for it, but she couldn't deny it. "I'll let you know if I get any more notes, but—"

"Or phone calls."

"Only if you agree to certain terms."

"Such as?"

"We keep our relationship strictly business. No more . . ." Her eyes moved to the sofa cushions, which still held the imprint of their bodies, then back to his. "No more of what just happened. No more physical contact between us at all, or the deal's off, and you can't tell my father or the police."

"Agreed."

C.J. extended her hand, then snatched it back the moment she remembered.

He grinned. "Of course, the deal's still on if you initiate the contact." He handed her a wineglass, then lifted his own. "Since we can't seal our bargain with a kiss, or a handshake, we'll have to drink to it." He downed the contents in one swallow, set the glass on the table, then rose and sauntered to the door. "I'll be in touch, figuratively speaking, of course."

She barely controlled the impulse to throw her glass at him.

C.J. FASTENED the small gold hoops in her ears and then stepped back to survey herself critically in the mirror. The muted shades of blue and gray in her glen plaid suit were a perfect match for the smudges under her eyes. She made a face at her reflection, then unzipped her makeup case and began to camouflage the telltale signs of her sleepless night.

When she was through, she gave herself a final scrutiny. What she saw in her reflection suggested neatness and competence, exactly what she needed to impress Jarvis Johnson's guidance counselor. But for the life of her she couldn't see anything to attract a man like Roarke Farrell.

If she had been asked to guess what kind of woman would appeal to him, she would have said someone a little flashier, a little more glamorous. Turning sideways, she frowned. Someone with more ample proportions. For one moment she found herself wishing for the kind of stunning beauty that would bring Roarke Farrell to his knees.

Then she shook her head and hurried out of the room. What was she thinking of? She wanted him out of her life, not falling at her feet. If he did, she'd just have to kick him out of the way. The image brought a smile to her face as she gathered up briefcase and dog and headed out of her apartment.

Twenty minutes later, C.J. turned into the parking lot at Monroe High. The building was square and unattractive. The roof was flat, the windows narrow and unadorned. In another setting, on acres of rolling lawns, its lines softened by ivy, it might have been more attractive. But here, in the center of the city, it was stark and ugly.

After cranking the front windows open a crack, she climbed out of the car. McBride whined a protest, then settled himself in the back seat. Next to the parking area, she could see an enclosed, cement playground. Two students leaned against the fence smoking. Another halfheartedly tossed an imaginary ball through a naked hoop. It reminded her of a prison yard. How could anyone discover a love for learning in a place like this? And yet it hadn't kept Roarke from following his dream. Of course, he wasn't a man who was easily discouraged. Without warning his words slipped into her mind. *I want to be your lover.* She swore under her breath as a shiver of anticipation ran up her spine.

When a car pulled into the space behind hers and a familiar voice called her name, she swore again. Had she conjured the man up simply by thinking of him? "What are you doing here? Our bargain doesn't give you the right to follow me."

"Whoa." Roarke raised his hands in surrender. "I'm here to see Jarvis Johnson. I swear. This is just a coincidence."

C.J. stared when he climbed out of his car. He was wearing jeans, worn white at the knees and seams, and a faded sweatshirt commemorating a long-ago sporting event. "You're here to see Jarvis dressed like that?"

"Correct."

"And just what do you want to see him about?"

"That's confidential. He's a witness for the state."

Her comment was short, but expressive. She turned and headed toward the back entrance to the school building. "If you're really here to see him, you'll have to wait your turn. I have a nine o'clock appointment with his guidance counselor." The old-fashioned double doors complained as she pushed through them.

"You won't have much luck with her," Roarke predicted. "She'll argue student confidentiality. And of course, she couldn't play any part in coercing a student to speak to you."

C.J. turned to glare at him. "You have a better plan?"

"I'm improvising."

C.J. snorted. "You look like a janitor."

"You look like a truant officer. These kids react negatively to suits."

C.J. compressed her lips and led the way into a glass-walled office. Behind a long counter, two women were typing. A third was stuffing slips of paper into mail slots. She turned to C.J. and Roarke the moment they entered.

Striking was the word that came to C.J.'s mind. She guessed the woman's age at about forty. Only a hint of gray could be seen in the ebony-colored hair she wore pulled back into a bun.

"I'm Mrs. Rinaldi. Can I help you?"

"Yes." They both spoke at once. Then Roarke gestured for C.J. to go first.

"I have an appointment with Mrs. Kingsley."

"I'm sorry, but she called in sick this morning. Perhaps I can—" A shrill bell interrupted. "Perhaps I can help you after the halls clear."

C.J. turned to see the corridor outside fill with students. Two young girls erupted into the office. One was leaning heavily on the other's arm.

"Mrs. Rinaldi, I can't go to gym class today. I have terrible cramps."

"You used that excuse last week, Janece."

"Please, I forgot my shoes."

Mrs. Rinaldi shook her head. "You know the rules. Report to the gym."

"I don't see why I have to do that," Janece whined. "Mrs. Kendricks will just give me an *F*. Why can't I go to study hall? I have a health test fourth period."

"Nice try, Janece. Next time bring your shoes."

C.J. noticed that the two girls gave Roarke an appreciative inspection as they left the room. His scruffy clothes did nothing to dampen his charm. To her surprise he excused himself and followed them out.

She turned back to Mrs. Rinaldi. "Some things never change. I tried the same thing whenever I had a chemistry test."

"I didn't even need a test as an excuse." Another bell shrilled through the school. "Why don't we go to my office and you can tell me why you made an appointment with Mrs. Kingsley." As C.J. followed the older woman, she recognized a familiar sensation. The sign on the door only confirmed her suspicion that she was being taken to the principal's office. She chose a chair and waited for Mrs. Rinaldi to take hers.

"I assume you're here about Tony Williams, Ms. Parker?" At C.J.'s surprised look, she continued. "I recognize you from the television news a week ago. I also recognized Mr. Farrell in spite of his disguise."

C.J. smiled. "I would appreciate anything you can tell me about Tony, but I came to ask Mrs. Kingsley about Jarvis Johnson. I'd like to talk to him."

Mrs. Rinaldi hesitated, picked up her pen and drew it through her fingers. "I'm not sure that I can help you with that. If I called him out of class, it might appear that I was pressuring him to talk to you."

Just what Roarke had predicted, C.J. thought, but she noticed that Mrs. Rinaldi's knuckles had whitened because of her grip on the pen. Switching to a new tack, she said, "What can you tell me about Tony?"

"He's dedicated to his studies, and to track, of course."

"He doesn't seem to care whether or not he's convicted."

Mrs. Rinaldi set her pen down. "He probably feels that his life is ruined either way."

"What do you mean?"

"Tony's dream was to win a track scholarship to college. It was his ticket out of here. With the trial and all the bad publicity, the scouts have lost interest."

"What if he's found innocent?" C.J. asked.

Mrs. Rinaldi shrugged. "The good news will be buried on page seven. Without some good PR to counteract the bad, he'll still be viewed as too much of a risk. Track isn't a big money sport like football or basketball."

"Do you think he did it?"

"Frankly I think what happened that night was a terrible accident. What's happened since is pure politics. A young man was seriously injured. The parents want revenge. The city and the college want the streets around the school to appear to be safe. So they'll put a bandage on the problem and send another young man to jail."

"Would you repeat that on the witness stand?"

"I'd shout it from the rooftop if it would do any good."

"Why won't you be equally frank with me about Jarvis Johnson?"

Mrs. Rinaldi leaned back in her chair and smiled. "I'll bet you're a very good lawyer. The problem is you're Tony's lawyer. It's your job to raise a reasonable doubt. I won't be a party to making Jarvis a scapegoat."

"I don't want to put the blame where it doesn't belong. But I am interested in the truth. I need to talk to both Jarvis and Larry Sawyer."

Mrs. Rinaldi rose. "I wish you the best, Ms. Parker, but I'm afraid I can't help you."

"I know about Jarvis's juvenile record."

"Where did you—" She stopped abruptly. "Never mind. Whatever you saw didn't give you the whole picture. The man who was principal before me had...problems controlling the student body. The police were called in quite frequently that year. Jarvis has a shakier family background than Tony. Plus he's the kind of kid who gets blamed for things. If there's disruption in a classroom, he's the one who'll get sent to the office. I know. He was in my class in sixth grade."

C.J. fished a card out of her pocket and placed it on the desk as she rose. "Jarvis has a good friend in you. I hope you can persuade him to come and see me. Larry, too. Tony claims that he can't remember everything that happened that night. It's possible that he's suffering from temporary amnesia. He could really use some help from his friends." She held out her hand and felt it warmly grasped. At the door she turned back. "Perhaps if you came with them when I question them?"

Mrs. Rinaldi nodded briefly. "I'll see what I can arrange."

When C.J. reached the doors leading to the parking lot, a tall, skinny kid with spiked hair pushed through them. Through the glass, she could see Roarke leaning against his car. She glanced over her shoulder at the boy. She'd have bet her last dime it was Jarvis Johnson. For a moment she debated going after him and decided against it. He might be more cooperative if Mrs. Rinaldi talked to him first.

Instead she strode across the parking lot to confront Roarke. "That was Jarvis Johnson, wasn't it? How did you get him out of class?"

"Janece offered to help."

"I'll just bet she did. What did you say to him?" She eyed him suspiciously. "You accused him of writing those notes, didn't you?"

"Sorry, that's confidential. But if you want to talk to him, I'll be glad to arrange a meeting."

"No, thanks," C.J. replied firmly. "Strong-arm tactics aren't going to get him to trust me. Besides, I don't need your..." She stopped herself just in time. Who was she kidding? If the District Attorney was going to deliver all his witnesses to her, she'd be a fool to object. "I don't need your help with Jarvis. How about arranging a meeting with Mr. and Mrs. Jasper and their son Peter?"

"All right."

C.J. stared at him. "Why would you do that?"

"What are friends for?"

"You're nuts." She turned and headed for her car. "While you're at it, I'd like to talk to Danny Jasper, too."

"Don't you think you're pushing it?"

She smiled. "What are friends for?"

Roarke laughed as he turned and lifted a box out of the back seat of his car. "I was going to deliver this to your office later. You can save me a trip." He opened the lid and lifted out a bouquet of lilies of the valley.

"They're to replace the flowers you nearly brained me with. Notice, I took the liberty of getting a smaller vase." The delicate porcelain cup fit neatly into the palm of her hand.

C.J. stared in silence as he climbed into his car and drove away. How in the world was she going to handle a man who made her mad enough to spit one minute and turned her knees to water the next?

7

C.J. STEPPED onto the elevator and pressed the button for the first floor. For one brief moment after her meeting with the Jaspers and their son Peter, she'd been tempted to see if Roarke was still in his office.

And then what would she do? Cry on his shoulder?

Kevin Wilson joined her just as the doors slid shut, then shifted his gaze uncomfortably to the front of the elevator.

She summoned up a smile. "Thanks for playing referee."

"Save your thanks for my boss. It was his party even though he skipped it. For what it's worth, you handled yourself very well."

"I can understand their rage. Especially Peter's. He must feel a certain responsibility for his brother's injury."

"Why do you say that?"

"It was his idea to go to Sutton Street that night. And he participated in the fight. What's the prognosis for his brother anyway? He must be making some progress."

Kevin's reply was caustic. "I guess you could call it that. He can actually recognize members of his family now."

"But Danny's young. Don't the odds favor his being able to recover whatever brain functions were damaged?"

"What do you think?" Kevin led the way out of the elevator. "You saw the X rays."

C.J. slowed to a stop. She was not likely to forget the X rays. Even now, if she closed her eyes, she would be able to see the pale, cloudy areas that indicated brain damage.

Kevin had disappeared through the revolving doors before she realized he had not answered her question.

Once on the street, she headed for her apartment. It was almost seven, too late to go to the office. Besides, she could work just as well at home. And who was she kidding? Roarke might be waiting for her at Patsy's Pub as he had been for the last three days. Why should she feel guilty just because she was looking forward to seeing him? All they did was talk.

Little by little she was learning things about him. He coached a soccer team on Saturday mornings, and he was fiercely proud of his two sisters. Moira ran her own restaurant in D.C. And Peggy taught nursery school in Baltimore.

As she walked past the windows at Patsy's, C.J. found herself searching the crowd for Roarke. Her hand was on the doorknob when she realized how much she wanted to see him. Needed to see him. What if he wasn't there?

Quickly she turned and walked through the parking lot to the back of the restaurant. She wasn't running away. She had to check on McBride. Doug had fashioned a leash for the dog that allowed him the run of a small courtyard off the kitchen.

But McBride wasn't running. He was lying enthralled at Roarke's feet having his belly scratched.

C.J. struggled not to be pleased and failed. She tried not to smile and gave up. When Roarke offered her a can of beer, she took a long swallow. It tasted bitter and cold, the perfect drink for a spring night that held the promise of summer. She sat down on a nearby bench and stretched her legs out in front of her. Tufts of grass and a few hardy dandelions had pushed their way through the cracks in the broken slate that paved the courtyard. Dusk was beginning to settle over the city. Still, the day's smells lingered. A light breeze carried the mingled scents of grilled meat and stale exhaust fumes. Through the open kitchen doors drifted the clatter of pots and pans and laughter.

"You're spoiling my dog," C.J. said.

"Me? Doug is the one who's feeling him scraps."

"So?"

"He's going to get fat."

C.J. took a swallow of beer. "McBride has it under control. He no longer touches that dry stuff you got for him."

"Smart dog. What did you think of the Jaspers?"

"Ken and Barbie meet middle age."

He grinned at the aptness of the description as C.J. continued. "They are the perfect suburban couple whose lives have been turned upside down by a horrible tragedy. They're both trying to cope. He's enraged. She's devastated."

"Is he angry enough to be your poison pen pal?"

Startled, C.J. turned to stare at him. "Are you serious?"

"Yeah." He hadn't known that he was going to ask her opinion, that he needed to ask her.

She considered the possibility for a minute, then shook her head. "Not his style. He's a bulldozer."

"What about the brother?"

C.J. frowned. "He's angry enough, especially at me for getting the postponement. But if he scares me off the case, the trial will only be delayed again." She turned to look at Roarke then. "And here I thought you were convinced that my client or one of his friends was to blame."

"I haven't eliminated them. Have you met with Jarvis yet?"

"Tomorrow. Mrs. Rinaldi is supposed to get back to me with the time. They'll all be coming to my office. Satisfied?"

Not by a long shot, he thought. She was only inches away, and he wanted to reach out and take her hand, link his fingers with hers. It had been days since he'd done anything as simple as take her arm. Instead he reached down to pet McBride.

C.J. watched his hand stroke the dog. His fingers were strong and lean. She remembered the way they had felt in her hair, on her skin. Sometimes demanding, other times gentle. As the images flashed into her mind, she felt her bones melting, her skin heating. She dragged her gaze away, then made the mistake of looking into his eyes. In their depths, usually so guarded, she could see quite clearly the carefully banked fire and everything it promised. The quick, bright explosion of pleasure that only he could bring her was waiting for her, only inches away. All she had to do was reach out and take it. The idea was so tempting, the impulse to give in so urgent, her fingers tightened on the beer can she was holding, bending the aluminum, and sending the liquid splashing onto her lap.

"Here." Roarke rescued the can and began to blot the wet spot with his handkerchief.

"No." Even through the layers of cloth, she could feel the warmth and the strength of his touch. C.J. made a grab for the hanky. But when her hand brushed against his, she jerked it back as if she'd been burned. Frantically she searched for something to say. Anything. Clearing her throat she said, "Have you decided yet whether or not you're going to try Tony's case yourself?"

Still holding the damp handkerchief, Roarke shoved his hand into his pocket. "Kevin Wilson asked me the same thing today. I didn't have an answer. It's the politically savvy thing to do. And I should step back and let Kevin prosecute the Sandra Hughes case."

"Afraid of a black mark on your win-loss record?" As soon as the words were out, she regretted them. "I'm sorry. I didn't mean that the way it sounded."

He smiled. "A few weeks ago you'd have believed that was true about me. I knew I'd change your mind about prosecutors."

She rose, suddenly feeling the need to move. McBride raised his head, then settled it once more between his paws. She walked the width of the small courtyard and then turned back to him. "I worked for a man in Chicago who cared only about winning." She linked her fingers together and twisted them as she began to pace. "I was naive. I thought that prosecutors, as officers of the court, would naturally put justice first. I was interviewing witnesses for one of my boss's cases, and I found someone who could clear a young man he had indicted."

Roarke had to fight the urge to go to her and take her hands in his. "He wasn't pleased, I take it?"

C.J.'s quick laugh held no humor. "Oh, he acted pleased enough. He even congratulated me before he had me reassigned to one of his colleagues."

"And behind your back he prosecuted the boy you knew was innocent."

C.J. stared at him. "That doesn't surprise you?"

Roarke shrugged. "Ambition does strange things to people. You didn't let him get away with it?"

C.J. shook her head. "I confronted him, but he told me that, in his opinion, my witness was not credible. So I turned the information over to the defense attorney. My ex-boss lost his case in a wave of publicity, and I resigned shortly after that."

"You were involved with him?"

"I'd gone out with him a few times. I admired him." She shrugged. "I broke my rule about not dating other lawyers, and I can't help wondering if I let my personal feelings blind me."

Roarke shoved aside the stab of jealousy. "So now you prefer to keep your work relationships and your personal relationships separate."

"It's for the best."

"Perhaps. But it's also impossible." He paused until she met his eyes directly. "We're already involved, C.J. And it's very personal. When this case is over, you'll have to deal with that. We both will."

He was right. She couldn't deny it, not when he could make her pulse throb by merely looking at her in that quiet, intense way. She chose the only solution she could think of. Retreat. Leaning down, she unfastened McBride's leash. "I have a lot of work."

"I can't interest you in one of Doug's hamburgers?"

She smiled. "I'll pass." He remained on the bench when she walked away. Since Monday, he hadn't offered to see her to the door. His restraint—no, more than that—his understanding that she needed to enter her apartment alone moved her.

Roarke counted to ten before he followed her. What propelled him forward was the image of C.J. climbing the stairs and walking alone down that dark hallway. He crossed the street and waited for the lights to go on in her apartment. Darkness had fallen while they had talked in the courtyard. Candles flickered in the windows of Patsy's Pub, spilling little pools of light onto the sidewalk. He started counting. When he reached twenty, C.J.'s apartment was still dark.

He told himself that he was being foolish and overprotective even as he walked toward the door of the Old Erie Gallery. After all, McBride was with her. In the foyer, he stopped trying to rationalize his actions and let whatever it was that had drawn him this far pull him up the stairs two at a time.

He was running when he reached the door of her apartment. She was standing just inside. Gripping her shoulders, he pulled her firmly around and into his arms. In the dim light, the wide loops of orange paint that streaked the walls and floors had a nightmarish quality. He felt the familiar quick surge of anger and shoved it ruthlessly away. But another emotion took its place.

Fear. His stomach was sick with it. If she'd been home when they'd come . . . His gaze followed the path of the orange paint where it had dripped down the walls to pool on the floor. He could easily picture C.J. lying in it.

Biting back an oath, he pressed her even closer. She didn't resist. But she didn't cling, either. And she wouldn't. There was strength here. He could feel it in the straightness of her back and in the fist that was balled against his chest. But there was a softness, too. One of his hands found its way up her back to the base of her neck. Very gently, as if she were a fragile piece of porcelain, he began to knead the knotted muscles.

She was so cold. He could feel it even through the wool of her jacket. He ran one hand up and then down her spine.

A noise from the kitchen made his muscles tense. He relaxed when McBride appeared in the archway. Then, still holding C.J. close, he reached to flip on the lights. On the walls, the paint circled the framed prints and stopped short of the bookshelves. On the floor, it came close but didn't touch her furniture.

He dealt with the second wave of anger as quickly as he had the first. But this time the emotion that it left in its wake was less easy to identify.

Desire? Was that what he was feeling? It wasn't like anything he had ever felt before. But he knew that he'd never wanted C.J. as much as he did right now. And not just for the pleasure that he was sure that they would bring to each other.

C.J. shivered and felt Roarke's arms tighten around her. In a moment she'd pull away. Just one more moment, she promised herself. But she was so cold. Odd that she hadn't noticed that until he'd drawn her into his warmth. For one more moment she let herself need it, depend on it.

Silly, it was only paint. Strange that she should feel so violated. But it would pass. And so would the fear that had knotted so tightly in her stomach. Very carefully, she concentrated on relaxing. Uncurling her fingers, she pressed them against Roarke's chest. Beneath her hand she could feel his heartbeat, sure and steady. As one minute stretched into the next, she felt her own gradually slow to match the rhythm of his. Then she drew in a deep breath. Odd that in such a short time, his scent should have become so familiar, so comforting. So necessary?

No, she was being foolish. It was just the reaction to what had happened. All week she'd been waiting for something. Anticipation was always worse than reality. Almost always.

When she drew back, she felt her chin gripped firmly.

"Are you all right?"

"Yes."

Her skin was still pale, but her eyes were clear when they met his. And she was steady when she turned to take a long look at the room. Roarke led her to the sofa and signaled McBride to her side.

"Stay here. I want to check the other rooms." When she started to rise, he placed a firm hand on her shoulder. "I don't think I'll find anything. Take a look. They've been very selective."

She was frowning when he returned. "A careful vandal?"

He was pleased to see that some of her color had returned. "You're not complaining?" He handed her a glass of wine and waited until she had taken a sip. "We have to call the police."

"I . . ." She paused and drew in a deep breath. "This may not be connected to the notes."

"True," he agreed amiably. "That's all the more reason to report it. What if it happens again to Sid and Doug or to the couple that runs the gallery?"

Her shoulders sagged in defeat. "How are we going to keep it from Paul?"

"Has it ever occurred to you that you're treating him exactly the way you don't want him to treat you?" She didn't look convinced. "I'll call a friend of mine, Lieutenant Mendoza. He'll do his best to keep a lid on it."

THE MAN ROARKE let into the apartment a half hour later was short and round and looked as if he had been sleeping in his clothes. He nodded briefly at C.J. when Roarke said her name and then bent over to test the nearest splash of paint with his finger. "Still tacky," he said as he wiped his hand on a wrinkled handkerchief. "Probably happened during the last two hours or so. What time does that gallery open?"

"Five o'clock," C.J. said.

"I'll check with them, see if they noticed anyone." He settled himself in the chair across from C.J. "I have a few questions about what Roarke told me over the phone."

"How about some coffee?" Roarke asked.

"It would save my life." Mendoza gave Roarke a brief smile before he flipped through a worn notebook to a blank page.

Roarke took his time measuring coffee and water into the automatic pot in the kitchen. He wanted to be with C.J., but he knew that his absence would allow her to talk more freely to Lieutenant Mendoza. Besides, he could trust his friend to probe until he got the answers he wanted.

When McBride rubbed against his leg, Roarke filled a bowl with water and set it on the floor. The dog whined again.

Roarke laughed. "You can't be hungry." He located mugs, spoons, cream and sugar and loaded them onto a tray, then leaned against the counter and listened to the murmur of voices from the next room.

How long would it take C.J. to realize that the reason for their hands-off agreement no longer existed? Whatever happened, he was not going to allow her to stay in this apartment alone tonight.

When the coffee was ready, he set it on the tray and headed back to the living room. "Help yourself," he said as he placed everything on the small table between them.

Mendoza waved him onto the couch. "Stay." The lieutenant loaded sugar and cream into a mug and took a careful sip before setting it down. "C.J. says you were out back when she arrived. You didn't see or hear anything suspicious?"

"No."

"Assuming the threats and this artistic escapade are related, we made a list of everyone connected with the Williams case." Mendoza passed him the notebook. "Any additions?"

Roarke skimmed through the names, noting his own as well as Kevin Wilson's and Paul's. "No," he said, handing it back.

"Two things bother me," Mendoza said as he glanced around the room. "The first is how neat this vandal has been. The second is motivation. The only thing to be gained by scaring you off the case is another delay in the trial. No one seems to want that."

"Suppose the purpose of all this is to rattle me so that I can't do a good job for Tony."

Mendoza grunted. "It's possible." He closed his notebook, slipped it into his pocket and then drained his mug. "I'll make some discreet inquiries and meet you at my office tomorrow at eleven. Bring the notes. I'll have the lab check for prints."

At the door, he stopped to inspect the lock. "They weren't professionals. Looks like they forced it with a screwdriver." He frowned at C.J. "You should invest in a good security system or at least a dead bolt. I'll alert the car that patrols this area, and we'll send a crew back to check for fingerprints. Is there someplace you can stay for the night?"

"She'll be staying with me," Roarke said.

C.J. opened her mouth to protest, but Roarke went on. "Either that or she'll stay with her boss, Paul O'Shaughnessy."

The lieutenant grinned. "I can recommend Roarke's place. The sofa bed's comfortable and the food's great!" He stepped into the hall and turned back. "Seriously, you shouldn't stay here until you tighten the security."

Roarke spoke the moment the door closed. "If you go to your father's house, you'll have to explain, so I'm taking you to my place tonight. We can argue about it all you want. But in the end you'll come, even if I have to drag you."

C.J. didn't doubt him, not for a minute. There was no mistaking the determination in his tone, but it was the hint of uncertainty that convinced her.

"Thanks. I'll pack my bag."

Disbelief. Amazement. She had the pleasure of seeing both on his face before she turned and walked into her bedroom.

C.J. STEPPED into the elevator with McBride in tow and pressed the button for the top floor. Her stomach plummeted even as the car began to rise. Nerves. The attack had begun on the ride to Roarke's place on Adams Street where a few deserted factories had been converted into luxury condominiums. Being greeted by a doorman certainly hadn't helped.

The doors slid open, and she stepped out onto a plush carpet. To the left, Roarke had said when he'd given her the key. He'd stayed behind to let the security people know that she'd be parking in the underground garage.

The door to his place had a dead bolt, of course. She stuck her tongue out at it before she inserted the key. Inside she flipped a wall switch and found herself in a huge barn of a room. It had to be twice, maybe three times the size of her apartment, and it was all one room. The outer wall was brick and broken by tall windows every few feet. The inner wall was lined with half-filled shelves and boxes. At the far end of the room, a Pullman-size kitchen was boxed in by a counter and stools. Closer to her, a sofa and two chairs faced a fireplace. The sofa bed? She fervently hoped not.

There had to be a guest room. Gripping her suitcase, she walked toward the far wall. Tucked into an alcove across from the kitchen she found a king-size bed flanked by two doors. One led to a bathroom, the other to a walk-in closet.

Too bad she hadn't thought to bring her sleeping bag. The closet would have held a family of five, she estimated. Or maybe she could sleep in the bathtub. Either way she was not going to panic simply because there weren't any walls or doors in Roarke's apartment. After all, they had an agreement.

Suddenly she sank onto the foot of the bed. Their agreement! What if he didn't see the need for it anymore?

In an effort to control the rising bubble of apprehension in her stomach, she began to unpack. Methodically she hung two suits in the closet and placed her shoes neatly beneath them, all the while trying to convince herself that Roarke had had no ulterior motive in bullying her into staying with him.

The third item she hung in the closet was a peach silk teddy. She stared at it in horror. Why on earth had she brought that? Subliminal urgings? She snatched it off the hanger, stuffed it into her suitcase and yanked out gray sweats.

A shower. She raced into the bathroom. Not to hide, but to think. A hot shower would clear her head.

THE EDGINESS Roarke had been feeling on the ride over doubled when he saw the door to his apartment standing open. He felt real panic when he stepped into the room and saw no sign of her.

"C.J.?" His heartbeat slowed when he reached the bedroom alcove and saw McBride. Then he heard the shower.

Control, he thought in disgust. He'd always prided himself on it. But he seemed to have little of it around

C.J. He pulled off his jacket as he walked toward the closet door.

The moment he saw her clothes hanging next to his, the jacket slipped from his hand, unnoticed. He breathed in her scent. He reached out to lay his hand on the shoulder of her suit and drew it slowly down the arm. Shaken, he tried to identify the flood of feeling that swept through him. Pleasure? Certainly. And a sense of rightness. He wanted them to be there. He wanted C.J. here in his home.

Slowly he dropped his hand to his side and backed up to sit on the bed. What had he gotten himself into, he wondered. He had desired women before this. But what he felt for C.J. was different. With any other woman he would have known what to do. But with C.J. he was never quite sure.

He could make her want him. But if he pushed her now, she might run, and he couldn't allow that. In order to protect her, he'd have to make sure she felt safe staying here with him. And that meant sticking to their agreement.

C.J. STEPPED OUT of the shower and toweled her hair into damp curls. After she pulled on her sweats, she rubbed the steam off the mirror and studied her reflection. She looked like one of Snow White's dwarfs. Dopey, the runt. All the better to scare off Prince Charming, she thought as she opened the door.

Roarke was standing in the kitchen area with his back to her. The sleeves of his shirt were rolled up. She could see the muscles in his arms tense, then relax as he chopped and tossed things into a pan. She remembered exactly how it felt to be held in those arms, and with the memory came a flare of desire. She waited for it to ebb, but she couldn't help wondering what would happen if she went to him and slipped her arms around his waist and laid her cheek against his back.

Impossible. Her hands clenched into fists at her sides. Even if she was tempted to throw her rules aside, she had to think of Tony. And more than that, she had to remember that the conflict in their careers wouldn't end with this particular case.

She walked to the counter and climbed up on a stool. He'd poured two glasses of wine. She took a swallow before she said, "There's something we need to talk about."

He turned to her then, amused that she'd brought the subject up. "You don't like omelets?"

"Omelets are fine."

"Then what's the problem?"

"Our agreement."

"Don't you think we've discussed that into the ground?"

"I just want to make it clear—"

"Spare me a repeat of the rules and regulations. I brought you here so that we could both get a good night's sleep. Notice the emphasis on sleep. You and McBride can share the sofa. I'll stay in my bed. Clear?"

"Yes."

He turned to the stove and then back to her as if he'd just thought of something. "One more thing." He moved toward the counter. "No agreement is going to change the fact that I want you." He saw something flicker in her eyes. Hope? Fear? "And you want me. We're going to be lovers. But I can wait."

His words held a promise as well as a threat, but C.J. was too grateful for the reprieve to argue. She swallowed, then said, "Is there anything I can do to help? With the omelets?"

He glanced around the confines of his work space and decided to forego the torturous pleasure. "Why don't you put on some music? Dinner will be ready in a minute."

C.J. hurried down the length of the room to the CD player. When she turned it on, jazz, low and brassy, poured out into the room. On the shelf she was facing were three framed diplomas. She frowned as she read the dates. Roarke had graduated from law school only four years ahead of her and eleven years after he'd finished high school.

"The omelets are ready."

She joined him at the counter and climbed onto a stool.

"Frowning like that will interfere with your digestion," he said. "What is it? I thought we had our problem all solved."

"You were only four years ahead of me in law school."

Amused, he shrugged. "Now you know my deepest, darkest secret."

"Why did it take you so long?"

"My father died when I was eighteen. All he left us was the bar. We had to make a go of the restaurant before there was any money for college."

"When my mother died, nothing changed for me. After the funeral, I went straight back to boarding school."

Not true, Roarke thought, watching her closely. The death of a parent made ripples in a life. Some were just harder to detect. "Life has a way of interfering with even the best laid plans. I still ended up where I wanted to be."

"No regrets?"

He smiled. "How could I regret any of it? My mother insisted on making me a full partner from the very beginning. Now that the restaurant is so successful that she's opening a second one, I can sit back and reap the rewards." He waved a hand. "I couldn't afford to live here on what an assistant District Attorney makes. Plus I learned to make an excellent omelet. Try it before it gets cold."

C.J. lifted the fork to her mouth and ate. "Delicious," she said as she took a second bite.

"See? If I'd taken the normal amount of time for college and law school, we might be eating a pizza or Chinese takeout."

C.J. said nothing. He might make light of the sacrifices he'd made, but it didn't lessen her admiration for him.

When they'd finished loading the dishes into the dishwasher, Roarke led the way to the couch at the end of the long room. "How about a game of Parcheesi?"

C.J. gave him an exasperated look. "You don't really play Parcheesi."

"I used to play it all the time with my sisters. I have a game in one of those boxes. Shall I get it out?"

"Spare me." She flopped on the couch, then shot a wary glance at the large book he lifted off a shelf.

"Shakespeare then. *Othello* is my favorite."

C.J. rolled her eyes and tried to dredge up what she knew about the play.

"Would you have taken his case?" he asked.

"Othello's?" She considered it for a minute, then shook her head. "He wouldn't have hired me. If I remember correctly, he kills himself. If he hadn't, he would have insisted on pleading guilty."

"How about Iago? Would you have defended him?"

"He didn't kill anyone. You would never have gotten an indictment."

"I'd go for conspiracy to commit murder."

C.J. thought for a minute. "I'd have to read the play again."

"Be my guest." Roarke pushed the book toward her. "You start, and we'll switch at the end of the first act."

"You're serious," C.J. said.

"It's either that or Parcheesi."

C.J. began reading the first act of *Othello*.

8

C.J. OPENED HER EYES to blinding sunlight. Startled, she sat up and immediately found herself out of the glare. The sun seemed to be aimed like a spotlight at the foot of the sofa where she'd fallen asleep. Another beam pinned McBride where he lay snoring a few feet away. It was not her sofa, not her room. Then she saw Roarke and remembered.

He was still fast asleep in the chair across from her. She drew her knees up and hugged them tightly while she studied him. His fingers brushed against the carpet. Next to them lay the volume of Shakespeare, still open. *Othello.*

Her lips curved in a smile. How far had they read? She couldn't recall much beyond the wedding in the first act. Funny how she'd forgotten that the play began with a love story. Othello had won Desdemona's heart with stories of his heroic deeds.

Ridiculous, wasn't it? To fall in love with a man because of the stories he told about his past? Very slowly, C.J.'s glance returned to Roarke's face.

Coffee. She rose and made her way carefully to the kitchen. A strong dose of caffeine was just what she needed to put everything into perspective.

While the water dripped slowly through the filter, C.J. punched numbers into the phone and checked the messages on her answering machine. The police would

want to know if anyone had called to gloat over the
paint job. But it was Mrs. Rinaldi's voice she heard.
Jarvis and Larry Sawyer would be arriving at her office
in less than an hour. C.J. let the tape run out as her mind
raced. There was no time to shower or change. She
didn't have the time to talk Roarke out of coming with
her, so she grabbed a piece of paper and scribbled him
a note. McBride rose as she passed him and followed her
to the door. Holding her breath, she pushed the dead
bolt back and let herself out.

C.J. STUDIED THE TWO young men sitting in front of her
desk. She had taken them through their statements
twice, asking them to move the colored dots around on
the map of Sutton Street, which covered her desk. Larry
Sawyer, the taller of the two, had been in perpetual
motion since he'd come through the door, but the second time through he'd relaxed enough to add details
that were not in his original statement. Jarvis Johnson,
on the other hand, had repeated his story verbatim both
times.

"I'd like to take you through it again," C.J. said.

"I don't want to be late for class," Jarvis drawled.

"I can always write you a pass," Mrs. Rinaldi said.

C.J. bit back a grin. "We don't have to start at the
beginning this time." She pointed to the dots, which
were clustered around the alley. "This is where the fight
started." She glanced at Jarvis. "Which boy did you
fight with?"

"We didn't introduce ourselves."

"Was it Danny?"

"No!"

The denial was immediate and explosive. At C.J.'s feet McBride raised his head and growled. She leaned over to pat his head. It was the first time that Jarvis's control had slipped. "How can you be so sure?" she asked. "You'd never met these boys before. How could you tell one from the other?"

Jarvis frowned. "The boy that got hurt was wearing an orange college sweater."

"That's right," Larry said. "Tony was wearing an orange sweatshirt, and the guy was after him to take it off because he didn't go to the college. They argued about it."

"So Tony was the only one who fought with Danny." She drew her finger from the cluster of dots on the map to the middle of the street where Tony had parked his car. "How do you suppose he got away from Danny long enough to get his bat out of the trunk?" She glanced up at the two boys. "It's more than a hundred yards away. What did Danny do while Tony was gone?"

"Maybe Danny followed him," Jarvis said.

"And they walked back to the alley before Tony hit him?"

For a moment there was silence. C.J. noted that Jarvis's hands were clenched, but his voice was flat and his eyes were shuttered when he spoke. "Why don't you ask Tony?"

"He can't remember. Tony's doctor thinks Danny must have landed a pretty good punch. Did either of you see it?"

Both boys shook their heads.

"If I put Tony on the stand, he won't be able to deny hitting Danny. That's why he needs your help."

Jarvis was still looking at the map as he rose from his chair. "I got nothin' more to say. Can we go now?"

"Sure," she said. "But if you remember anything else . . ." The boys were out the door before she could finish. Turning to Mrs. Rinaldi, she said, "Jarvis knows more than he's saying."

"It's possible."

"He may feel more comfortable talking to you about it."

Mrs. Rinaldi smiled. "I'll see what I can do."

"Thanks."

For a time after her office had emptied, C.J. frowned at the map. McBride stood next to her with his chin resting on the desk. She patted his head absently. "Something's different, boy. Something about the dots—the blue ones are Tony and his friends. And the orange ones are the college boys . . ." Suddenly her expression cleared. "They're not evenly matched anymore. See. It's two against one up here. And it's the same down here in the street." She patted the dog again. "It's not much, but it's something. Jarvis could tell me more. Let's hope he will."

ROARKE RECOGNIZED JARVIS and Mrs. Rinaldi the moment they walked down the steps. Swearing under his breath, he slammed on his brakes and pulled to a stop at the curb across the street. He forced himself to wait until they were out of sight before he got out of his car. C.J. was safe, he told himself. Mrs. Rinaldi's presence guaranteed that. Slowly the panic that had been building from the moment he'd awakened to an empty apartment was replaced by anger. At himself? At C.J.? He didn't stop to analyze it as he tore up the steps of the building. Finding her leaning over her desk talking to McBride only added fuel to the fire.

"What the hell do you think you're doing?"

She turned to face him, but before she could speak, he yanked her into his arms. Her lips parted beneath his as he ran his hands over her quickly, pressing her close, reminding himself of her softness, her strength. The moment she melted against him, his anger drained away, and something else began to build. Not passion this time, not anything quite that simple. Moments ago he'd wanted nothing more than to throttle her. Now he wanted to go on holding her forever.

Even after the kiss ended, C.J. kept her arms around him, resting her head under his chin. She'd seen the fury in his eyes when he'd burst into the office. She'd tasted his fear and felt it in the desperate touch of his hands. Then she'd sensed the change, the gentling. No, more than that. The longing? Was that why her anger hadn't built to match his as it always had before? Was this what it felt like to love someone? Madness, she thought. Where had it gotten poor Desdemona? For one more moment she held him tight.

When they finally drew apart, they stared at each other for a moment. Roarke spoke first. "I'm sorry."

It wasn't what she wanted to hear, but C.J. managed a nod. Leaning back against her desk, she watched him pace. He wore jeans and a sweatshirt, running shoes, but no socks. He hadn't shaved or combed his hair. She wanted to stroke her fingers through it and smooth it off his forehead. But when he pinned her with a look, she saw that the storm was once again raging in his eyes.

"You could have left me a note," he said.

"I did."

"Where?"

"On the pad next to the phone."

"Oh. I didn't think to look there."

For the first time she noticed how tired he looked. "I'm sorry. I . . . would you like some coffee?"

"Coffee?" He almost laughed. What he wanted was her. He glanced at her desk and thought about clearing it with one sweep of his arm. He could make sure that she never sat at it again without thinking of him. He shook his head to clear it.

"Coffee," C.J. repeated. "You know, the black stuff that tastes terrible and wakes you up in the morning?"

"Ah, yes. Coffee." He walked quickly toward the door, giving the desk and C.J. a wide berth. "Why don't we have a cup back at my place. Unless you plan to work in your sweats."

C.J. stared at his back as he left her office. Something had changed. She couldn't for the life of her figure out what. Except that they'd apologized to each other. Shaking her head, she nudged McBride from his prone position and hurried after him.

OUTSIDE, THE RAIN FELL in spurts and stops for the third day in a row. Inside, C.J. sat at her desk, doodling on a legal pad and waiting for Lieutenant Mendoza to return her call.

If someone had told her that she could make it through four days living with Roarke without friction, she wouldn't have believed it. She stared at the window and watched a drop of rain wind a path down the pane. Four days and four nights and they hadn't argued once except over whether or not Iago could be tried for murder. Even then, they'd agreed to table the argument indefinitely. After all, they both had real legal battles to worry about.

Roarke was very considerate. She printed the word in capital letters on her legal pad. He allowed her to use the bathroom first in the morning. And in the evening when she was ready for bed, he took McBride for a very long walk. On Saturday, he'd introduced her to his soccer team, the Blazing Blue Demons. A more aptly named group of nine-year-olds she'd never met.

All in all, he'd been a perfect gentleman. She wrote the word and enclosed it in a heart. Except for that one lapse when he'd kissed her right here in the office, he'd kept to their agreement. She pierced the heart with a huge arrow.

He was treating her like a . . . what? She drew the pencil through her fingers as she searched for the right word. Companion? Housemate? Little sister? The pencil snapped in two, bringing McBride to his feet in a flash. Head cocked, tail wagging, the dog faced her across the desk. She tossed the eraser half of the pencil the length of the room and watched him scramble to retrieve it.

When he brought her the wet prize, she scratched behind his ears. "He's treating me like a sister. It's nice. It's safe." She sighed. "It's what I thought I wanted. It's what I ought to want." While she talked, she scribbled absently on her pad. There was nothing she could fault Roarke for. The struggle was within herself, between her goals and her needs, between what she'd planned and what she desired. Her eyes suddenly focused on the drawing she had made. She held it up for McBride to see and said, "If I'm so sure of what I want, why am I drawing Roarke Farrell with a noose around his neck?"

At Paul's crack of laughter she glanced up to the connecting doorway. "A noose around his neck, huh? How does it work? Like some kind of voodoo?"

"Don't I wish." C.J. quickly flipped the pad over.

"That bad?" Paul crossed to the desk and studied the map of Sutton Street. "No breakthrough yet?"

C.J. shook her head. "Jarvis Johnson is the key. I've been hoping he'll confide in Mrs. Rinaldi. He seems to trust her."

"Maybe he needs a nudge."

C.J. glanced at the phone. "I'm working on it. Anything new on the Sandra Hughes case?"

Paul smiled. "As a matter of fact, I just got a call from Sam Hillerman. He's found a witness, thanks to your suggestion. A cleaning lady. Works for one of those franchises—magic maids, merry maids, whatever. She just happened to be driving by when a black sedan pulled out of the Days' driveway."

"That's great!"

"I agreed to meet Sam for a drink, but I don't have my car."

"Take mine," she said.

"Can you join us?"

"No." She glanced at the phone again. "I'm hoping for that 'nudge' we talked about."

Paul's smile faded. "You won't ..."

"Take any risks," C.J. finished for him. "No, I won't. You, on the other hand, are taking your life in your hands now that you're driving my car."

Paul groaned. "Don't remind me."

"When is the garage going to set yours free?"

"Damned if I know!" Paul was still muttering about stupid mechanics when he shut the door of her office.

C.J. leaned down to pat McBride's head. "I think we're making progress with him, fella." She reached to push the button as her intercom buzzed.

"Lieutenant Mendoza is on line three," said Ruth. "And Paul has just invited me to have a drink with him. Do you need me for anything?"

"No." C.J. was already reaching for the phone. "Go on. Have a good time. Inspector?"

There was a moment of silence before the gruff voice came over the line. "Ms. Parker, I'm returning one of your four, no five phone calls. Have you received another threat?"

"No, I want to know what you found out about those prints."

"Hold on. I've got another call. It may be an emergency."

His emphasis on the last word made C.J. wince. The police lab had lifted several unidentified prints from her apartment. Tony had been immediately cleared, and Mendoza had balked at first when she'd asked him to check the prints in Jarvis's sealed file. He'd only been slightly less reluctant to try for a match with any unidentified prints that had been lifted from the baseball bat. C.J. paced to the window. The phone cord prevented her from going any farther. In the parking lot below, Paul stalled her VW twice before he pulled out onto the street. The traffic was heavy, and a blue station wagon nearly hit another car as it wedged its way into a space behind Paul at the light. There was something familiar about the wagon, but before she could recall where she'd seen it before, Lieutenant Mendoza came on the line again.

"Ms. Parker, Jarvis Johnson did not leave any prints in your apartment. Nor is there any evidence that your anonymous interior decorators handled the baseball bat that injured Danny Jasper. However, at some point Jarvis certainly had his hands on that bat. Long enough to leave three good prints."

C.J. sank into her chair.

"You still there, Ms. Parker?"

"Yes. Thank you, Inspector."

"Don't mention it. And I mean that literally. My superiors would not be happy to learn that I've been digging into a sealed file. And none of this would be admissible in court."

"I won't breathe a word, and thanks again." C.J. replaced the receiver and sat staring thoughtfully at the blue-and-orange dots on her map. Did she have enough to nudge Jarvis? He was definitely lying. According to the map in front of her, Larry Sawyer was at the mouth of the alley fighting two of the college boys, and Jarvis was with Tony and Danny in the street. Either Jarvis had lied about not fighting with Danny, or he had been the one to get the bat out of the car. The prints supported the latter scenario. With a sigh, C.J. folded up her map and stuffed it into her briefcase. It was time to talk to Jarvis again.

"Time to go home," she said to McBride and followed him as he raced for the door. Once out on the street, she found herself walking toward Roarke's apartment. Was she beginning to think of it as home? She turned toward Patsy's Pub. Maybe in her own place, surrounded by familiar things, she could think more clearly about Roarke.

It wasn't until she was in the foyer that she remembered she'd promised Roarke she wouldn't come back alone. But she wasn't alone, she reasoned: she had McBride. When she reached the top of the stairs, she was stunned to see her furniture lining the walls of the hallway and Gina standing in the open doorway of her apartment.

"Oh, no. You're not supposed to be here. We wanted it to be a surprise," Gina said.

"A surprise?" C.J. glanced into her apartment, then turned and stared. The walls were free of paint. The floor gleamed with a fresh coat of varnish.

Gina was wringing her hands. "Roarke will have a fit."

"Roarke did this?"

"No, it was my idea. I wanted to find a way of paying you back for saving my greenhouse. I arranged for the men who are working on my restaurant to come over. Please don't be angry."

"Angry?" C.J. felt the burning at the back of her eyes and blinked. Her gaze dropped to the security alarm box near the door. She ran her fingers over the buttons. "This was Roarke's idea."

"Well, yes. In fact, he was rather adamant about it, and one of my contractors is very clever with electrical things. It's really for the best. A young woman living alone—" Gina broke off when she saw the tear run down C.J.'s cheek. "Oh, my." Gina drew her over to the couch. "What's the matter?"

C.J. shook her head as she sank into the cushions. How could she explain when she didn't understand herself? Her apartment was beautiful. Why did she feel so miserable? "It's all ready for me to move back in then?"

"It was all set on Sunday, but Roarke insisted on a third coat of varnish for the floor. And with this rain, it takes such a long time for it to dry."

"It's beautiful, really."

"But you hate it. Roarke warned me that you were very independent, that you'd prefer to handle everything by yourself. But I thought . . . I just wanted to do something to thank you."

C.J. took the older woman's hands in hers. "I don't hate it. I love it. It's just such a surprise."

Gina looked into C.J.'s eyes, searching for reassurance. "And you're not angry with Roarke for the security system? He can't help wanting to protect the people he cares about. I know it can be annoying. He used to drive his sisters nuts. I blame it on the way his father was killed."

"Killed? All Roarke told me was that he was eighteen when his father died."

"My husband was shot by a man who broke into the tavern after-hours. We never thought about security systems in those days. We just locked our doors."

C.J. tightened her grip on Gina's hands. "It must have been terrible for you."

Gina nodded. "But it was worse for Roarke. He was so angry. At first I didn't notice. He stepped into his father's shoes so easily, calling the police and arranging for the funeral. And later I blamed his anger on the results of the trial, and the fact that my husband's murderer went free."

A wave of empathy washed over C.J. leaving her stunned. She knew too well what it was like to lose a parent. But her mother hadn't been the victim of a violent crime or a failure of the criminal justice system. "How did it happen?"

"Who knows? Roarke blamed it on the District Attorney for doing a sloppy job. But more than anything he blamed his father for being careless, for leaving us that way."

"But why? It wasn't his father's fault."

"No. But then our feelings are seldom logical, are they? And the deeper Roarke's feelings run, the more he tries to control them."

C.J. began to play back the events of the past week in her mind. Was that what he'd been trying to do? Control his feelings for her? She recalled his routine, a run in the morning, a fast escape into his bedroom after dinner and a late-night walk with McBride until she tucked herself into bed on the sofa. Was he trying to protect her again?

For the first time since she'd walked through the door, she began to smile. She thought of his words to her that first night in the kitchen. *We're going to be lovers. But I can wait.* He'd kept his word. He'd even made it possible for her to move back into her apartment in time for the trial. She rose from the couch and started for the stairs. Maybe he could protect her from his feelings, but not from her own.

Suddenly she remembered Gina and McBride. She turned and saw them both staring at her curiously. "I have to thank Roarke," she explained, moving to pick up the dog's leash. "And thank you, too, Gina," she added as she hurried away.

ROARKE PACED back and forth in the small kitchen area and glanced at his watch. Seven o'clock. He grabbed a wooden spoon and stirred the chili that was simmering over a low flame. He'd phoned her office three times since six o'clock. The walk would take her twenty minutes, thirty if she decided to crawl on her hands and knees. He jerked open the refrigerator door and stared at the salad. It was just as ready as it had been at six-thirty.

Patience, he told himself, but he was swearing as he paced to the window and stared out at the falling rain. If he wanted a future with C.J., he had to convince her that he trusted her to take care of herself. How many times had he told himself that since she'd moved in?

He strode to the fireplace to light the kindling he'd laid earlier. In seconds, flames leapt up to devour the larger logs, hissing, crackling. He barely had time to replace the screen before a spark flew against it. The fire reminded him of C.J. Explosive and unpredictable. If she were a case, he'd rely on his instincts and improvise. But he had little doubt where improvisation would lead with C.J. He swore again at the images that filled his mind and moved toward the bathroom. One more cold shower would at least keep him in the apartment for ten more minutes.

C.J. CAUGHT the spicy scent of food the moment she stepped off the elevator. Roarke was home. She pressed a hand against her stomach to quiet the nerves that had begun to build on the walk over. Her plan was simple really. There was only one way to convince him that he didn't have to protect her from his feelings or her own. Her hand trembled slightly as she turned her key in the

lock and pushed open the door. The apartment was empty.

McBride headed straight for the fire, pulling her with him. "Smart dog," she said, leaning over to unfasten his leash. Then she backed up to avoid a quick shower as he shook himself off. By the time she had slipped out of her raincoat, the dog had wandered off to the kitchen in search of food. She could almost envy him. His needs were so simple. Food, warmth, affection. Why did her own seem so complicated?

C.J. added another log to the fire and watched the flames leap. Loving Roarke would be like that, bursts of passion, flashes of heat. Like the log, she would run the risk of changing, losing part of herself. Perhaps she already had.

Roarke stepped out of the shower and reached for his watch. Seven-twenty. He dried himself, then hooked a fresh towel around his waist. She had to be here. If she wasn't . . . Leaving the thought unfinished, he grabbed his jeans and opened the bathroom door. The timer on the stove was beeping. He barely missed colliding with C.J. on his way to shut it off. Relief was mixed with anger. "Where the hell have you been?"

C.J. tried to speak and found she couldn't. The sight of Roarke wearing nothing but a towel wiped her mind clean.

"You're wet." He handed her the jeans he was carrying.

C.J. stared at them. "You want me to change into these?"

Roarke's gaze dropped to the jeans, then to the towel he was wearing. "Damn!" Grabbing his pants, he said, "I'll get you a dry towel."

C.J. stared after him as he disappeared into the bathroom. He was rattled. The great Roarke Farrell was actually rattled. For the first time since she had left her apartment, she began to relax. She shut off the timer and stirred the chili. When McBride brushed past her, she turned to watch him settle himself on Roarke's bed. From the very first night, he had slept with Roarke. Once again, C.J. found herself envying the simplicity of her pet's needs. When the door to the bathroom opened, she busied herself opening a bottle of wine.

He was standing on the other side of the counter when she turned around. In silence, she took the towel he gave her and handed him a glass of wine. The guarded look in his eyes told her that he'd recovered some of his control. But the tension was still there in his shoulders. He hadn't bothered with a shirt. Her gaze traveled down his bare chest to the countertop. Had he remembered to pull on his jeans? Before her thoughts could scatter again, C.J. plunged into speech. "It's beautiful. My apartment, I mean. I stopped by on my way home. I mean here." When she saw the anger in his eyes, she rushed on. "I know I promised not to go there alone. But I didn't. I had McBride, and Gina was there. It was so kind of her. Of you, too. Of course, I'll pay you back for the security system."

"Fine. I'll send you a bill." Roarke took a swallow of his wine. Even across the width of the counter he caught the floral scent of her hair. He had to force his fingers to relax their hold on the glass when he set it on the counter. Did she have any idea how much it was costing him not to touch her? In desperation, he moved to the stove. "Are you hungry?"

But when he picked up the spoon to stir the chili, C.J. took it out of his hands and twisted the flame off. "We can eat later."

When he still said nothing, she reached out to run her hand over the smooth skin on his shoulder.

Roarke searched for words and found none. A new experience, and not the first she'd given him. He gave in to the urge to touch her, just the ends of her hair. The curls, still damp from the rain, felt impossibly soft. He drew one finger along the line of her jaw. Her skin was cool. He ran his hand down her arm and linked his fingers with hers. "Are you sure?"

Smiling, she drew him with her toward the fire. She wanted him. It was as simple as that. Inevitable. If she was making a mistake, she would willingly pay the price.

Roarke sank to his knees and drew her down so that she was facing him. Their hands were still joined, but he didn't pull her closer. For a moment he simply looked at her. It was enough to interfere with her breathing.

The firelight played over his skin, turning it a golden bronze and making him look like some pagan god. A sudden change in the the direction of the wind outside sent a puff of smoke into the room. C.J. thought of incense and sacrificial offerings.

When he finally reached to touch her, it was only to unfasten the thin, gold hoops at her ears. As his fingers brushed along her cheek, he watched the tremor move through her. Lit only by the fire, her skin looked so delicate. And yet there was an underlying strength. Was it the contrast that pulled at him so?

Her necklace attracted him next. He moved one finger along it, then lifted it and retraced its path along her throat. He felt the quick scramble of her pulse and hunger surged through him. But for the moment it was enough to watch pleasure darken her eyes.

Barely touching her, he eased the jacket down her arms. C.J. watched through half-closed lids as he folded it and placed it neatly next to her earrings. Her blouse was next. One by one, he unfastened the buttons and slipped it off her shoulders. Just seeing him handle her clothes made her feel weak, wanton. To steady herself, she raised her hands to his chest. His skin was hot, his heartbeat quick. Her own accelerated to match its rhythm.

He took her hands and pressed his mouth to the center of each palm before gently lowering them to her sides.

"Roarke?" His name came out on a sigh.

He brushed his fingers across her lips. "I've waited so long to touch you." Very slowly he traced the silk of her teddy where it curved along the top of her breast. "So long."

Leaning over, he followed the path his hand had taken with his mouth. Her skin heated beneath his lips, adding new subtleties to her taste, tempting him to explore further. He drew in endless flavors as he sampled the smooth, taut skin of her shoulder, the satiny softness of her arm. Then he moved lower, until through thin silk, he drew her nipple into his mouth.

C.J. sagged against him as a thousand little sparks of pleasure rocketed through her. Gripping his shoulders, she held him tight as he eased her back onto the carpet. Reality blurred into a series of heightened sensations—the press of his strong fingers on her waist and thighs as he stripped off her skirt, the scrape of his nails on her arch as he shoved at her shoe.

I'm burning, she thought as her mind began to spin. She could feel the flames leap and lick along her skin just as clearly as she could see them flickering red and hot against her eyelids. His mouth moved over her bringing no relief. It felt like a branding iron, leaving its mark on every part of her.

Very slowly, Roarke journeyed up her body to her mouth. Still, he resisted the temptation to explore its moist treasures. Threading his fingers through her hair, he whispered against her lips, "Tell me what you want."

"You. I want you."

"How do you want me?"

Images swirled through her mind. "Inside of me. Now." But when she reached for him, he took her hands and held them in one of his above her head.

"Soon." Roarke found it took all of his control to draw away. She lay before him in the glow of the fire wearing only a swatch of cream-colored silk and a thin gold necklace. She was his. The long days and nights of the past week had the need pounding through his veins. But there was more pleasure he wanted to give her.

He traced the lace trim of her teddy as it rode high on her hips, then dipped low between her legs. When he slipped his fingers beneath the silk to tug the snaps loose, she arched against his hand and moaned his name. His mind clouded as his fingers gripped the edge of her panty hose and dragged them down her legs.

His hands weren't gentle now as they raced over her, nor was his mouth when it covered hers. She tasted desperation as his tongue tangled with hers. She felt urgency when his fingers traced a path up her thigh. Desire became razor-sharp as they slid into her heat.

Closer. The word spun through her mind as she thrust against him, inviting, begging. She ran her hands over his back, then dragged them to his waist and yanked at the waistband of his jeans. Together they struggled with the denim, shoving it out of the way. And then she found him, closed her fingers around him and arched upward, demanding.

The last of his control melted away as he slipped into her. All he knew was the texture and scent of her skin, the searing heat of her body as it drew him deeper and enfolded him. Sensations blurred together as their bodies became fused into one, and when he began to move, Roarke felt a part of himself flow into her.

C.J. cried out his name as the first sure thrusts of his hips sent an explosion ripping through her. He gave her no time to recover. Together they moved, one breath, one heartbeat, one rhythm, until they reached a shattering release.

Afterward Roarke watched the fire gleam in her hair as she lay snuggled in his arms. The apartment was quiet except for the sound of the rain and McBride's snoring. He could feel the beat of her heart at his chest, the warmth of her breath each time she exhaled. He could have lain there forever.

He loved her. It had taken him long enough to put that word to what he was feeling, to what he had been feeling for some time. He knew better than most the power of words. If you didn't say it, it didn't really exist. Now it did, for him at least. The next step would be to see that it existed for C.J., too. And that would take time. He would have to find the patience somehow.

For the first time in a week, C.J. felt at peace. She drew in a breath and smelled his scent. She ran her tongue along her lip and tasted him. Turning slightly, she found him watching her, a wary expression in his eyes.

With a smile, she reached out and touched his cheek. "Having second thoughts, Farrell?"

"Nah. I'm still trying to formulate first ones. I think the rational side of my mind shut down when you walked in the door tonight." He tucked a curl behind her ear. "You're full of surprises."

"You seem to be able to handle anything I come up with."

He ran a hand slowly down her side and then up to settle under her breast. "I'm at my best when I'm improvising."

She could feel her heart begin to thud under his palm. "I prefer to plan everything out." She slid her hand from his cheek down his chest until her fingers rested light and low on his stomach. "One step at a time."

"Ahh," he breathed as her fingers closed around him, and his mind began to cloud. "You favor the direct approach."

As C.J. felt the effect her touch had on him, she had to put more effort into following the thread of their conversation. "It has its merits."

"Still, you shouldn't overlook alternative solutions." In one quick move, he rolled onto his back and lifted her.

C.J. laughed, then gasped when he slipped swiftly and deeply inside her. Her eyes widened as her hunger built with a speed and intensity that shocked her. The first two thrusts sent her immediately spinning back into a world of sensations. Her skin burned where his fingers pressed into her hips. She grasped his shoulders to keep herself in position and watched his face. The instant his features tightened in concentration, her own pleasure exploded. Fighting the pressure of his hands, she increased the rhythm and took him with her until she once more heard his cry of satisfaction.

9

"I KNOCKED, but you didn't answer."

With a guilty start, C.J. stopped singing a little song in her head and looked up to find Ruth standing in front of her.

"I also buzzed. Mrs. Rinaldi is on line two."

"Sorry."

Ruth shook her head on the way to the door. "You're as bad as your father when you get all wrapped up in a case."

C.J. felt another stab of guilt as she glanced down at the map covering her desk. Her thoughts had been on the surprise she was planning for Roarke. And it wasn't the first time she'd caught herself daydreaming when she should have been working. She reached for the phone. "Mrs. Rinaldi?"

"I'm sorry I didn't get back to you sooner, but I haven't had any luck with Jarvis. He hasn't been in school all week."

"The trial starts next Wednesday. I need to talk to him before that."

"You might be able to catch him tomorrow. He handles the sound for Monroe High's Jazz Band, and they'll be playing at the Downtown Committee's Fair." Mrs. Rinaldi paused for a moment. "Unless you have other plans? I know it's a Saturday."

"As a matter of fact, I'll be at the fair, grilling hot dogs with the Blazing Blue Demons."

"Oh?"

"Mr. Farrell coaches a soccer team, and he asked me . . . it's a long story."

Mrs. Rinaldi laughed. "I've heard that he's a very persuasive man."

"Well, you'll have no trouble finding me. I'll be surrounded by blue shirts and burnt franks."

"You're on your own this time. Since Jarvis seems to be avoiding me, I'm going to keep my distance. Good luck."

"Thanks. I'll need it."

"You got a minute?" Paul stood in the doorway.

"Sure." C.J. hung up the phone. "What's up?"

"I'm not sure how to ask you."

C.J. stared at her father. Paul O'Shaughnessy unsure of how to phrase a question?

"I called you last night. When I got the machine, I tried to track you down at Patsy's. Sid told me you were out with Roarke."

C.J. held her breath, wondering what was coming next. So far Paul hadn't found out about the vandalism or her current living arrangements. She wasn't sure which would upset him more.

"Has Roarke ever asked you about the Hughes case?"

"No." She released the breath she'd been holding. "We've never discussed it."

"You're sure?"

"Are you asking me if I've been indiscreet?"

Paul frowned and began to pace. "No. Of course not."

"Then what?"

"I just finished interviewing that witness Sam found, the cleaning lady I told you about. She claims she signed a statement for the Farberville police a few days after the murder."

"They knew someone could corroborate Sandra's story?"

"Seems so."

It took C.J. only a moment to sift through the possibilities. "You don't think Roarke knew about it and suppressed the statement on purpose?"

"I don't want to believe that."

"Then don't. Roarke would never do something like that just to get a conviction."

He stopped at her desk. "You sound very sure of that."

"I am." She reached for the phone. "I'll call him right now and ask him to find out what happened."

"No. You can't say anything about this. If you're right and he doesn't know anything about the statement, then I have a surprise witness. She could win this case for us."

And lose the election for Roarke. C.J. pushed the thought aside. "You're right. And I know I'm right about Roarke."

Paul moved toward the connecting door to his office, turned back. "Ruth tells me you start jury selection on Wednesday. I could be there in the morning, if you'd like. But Roarke and I are scheduled for more preliminary motions on the Hughes case Thursday."

"Then Roarke has decided not to try Tony's case?"

"Oh, he'll be there when he can. In second chair. You didn't know?"

"The last time I asked, he hadn't decided."

Paul studied her for a moment. "It's a risky move, trying the Hughes case. That's why I brought it up. I think he might have something up his sleeve. But this

is good news for you. You'll have an easier time with
Kevin Wilson."

She managed a smile, but it faded the moment her
father closed the door to his office. It took her less than
three minutes to load her briefcase and head out the
door.

FORTY-FIVE MINUTES LATER, C.J. backed through the
door of Roarke's apartment, picnic basket in one hand
and McBride's leash in the other. After releasing the
dog, she staggered with the basket to a table. Doug
must have packed more than she'd ordered.

When she opened it, she saw a yellow rose lying on
a snowy white tablecloth. She picked it up and inhaled
its scent while she lifted the cloth. Nestled across from
a stack of neatly labeled containers was a bottle of
champagne in a thermal jacket and two glasses. Perfect. With a sigh she closed the lid again. At least it
should have been perfect. Still carrying the rose, she
began to walk back and forth across the floor.

Roarke found her pacing, lost in her thoughts, when
he let himself in a short time later. For a moment he
leaned against the door and simply took in the scene.
McBride lay in one of the rectangular shaped splashes
of sun that poured through the windows. As C.J.
stepped over him, the light shot through her hair in-
tensifying the reddish gold color. She was wearing it
clipped back at the sides, but it fell loose in the back.

It was good to be home, Roarke thought as his gaze
wandered down the length of the room. He'd moved in
more than two years ago, and he couldn't remember
ever thinking of it as home before. He glanced back at
C.J. Whatever she was thinking about had her completely absorbed. She was like that when she made

love, too. Totally focused. His gaze moved down the neat little suit to her slender legs as he wondered how long it would take him to shift her train of thought.

He was halfway to her when he noticed her brush the yellow rose across her cheek. "Who gave you the rose?" he asked.

She jumped and whirled around. "I didn't hear you come in."

"The rose. Who gave it to you?" He hadn't known before that jealousy could burn.

She glanced down at the flower. "Doug. I asked him for it." She held it out to him. "It's for you."

Pleasure erased the jealousy. "For me?" But when he reached for it, she snatched it back.

"It was. Now, I'm not so sure."

He noticed the wicker basket then and walked over to it. "What's this?" He lifted a plastic container. "Deviled eggs?"

C.J. frowned. "It's a picnic."

He smiled. "For me?"

Her frown deepened into a scowl.

"What's the problem?"

"You are."

When he moved toward her, she stepped back. "No. We have to talk about this."

"Okay." He sat on the arm of the sofa and studied her, recalling how absorbed she'd been when he'd first come in.

She waved the rose at him. "You're distracting me. Tony's trial starts next Wednesday. It should have my undivided attention. And I spent time today, planning a picnic."

"A good plan. Be a shame to waste it."

"Then Paul told me that you're taking the second chair in Tony's case."

Roarke's eyes narrowed. "And that's a problem?"

She threw a hand up in the air. "Of course it is. I should have known about it. My brain is so fuddled since I moved in here with you that I forgot to ask! And that's not all. I want to know why you're not trying his case." She closed the distance between them and grabbed one of his lapels with her free hand. "If you decided not to because of some misguided and totally unforgivable desire to protect me, so help me . . ."

She was magnificent like this, he thought. All fired up and ready to fight him to the finish. He tried to concentrate on her implied question. "You want to know if my decision had anything to do with you?"

She noticed that she was still gripping his jacket and dropped her hand. "Yes."

"Well, it didn't and it did."

She pointed the rose at him. "Spell it out for me."

"I think it's true to say that if I hadn't met you, I would be trying the Williams case."

She made a noise, but Roarke held up a hand. "Let me finish. There didn't seem to be anything wrong with accepting the publicity for an easy conviction, and I figured I could always supervise Kevin during the Hughes trial. But watching the way you were approaching Tony's defense reminded me of the first few years I practiced law. And I remembered why I wanted to become District Attorney in the first place. I wanted to make the system work better. The only way I can do that is to make sure that the best possible prosecution goes up against the best possible defense. So I decided to handle the Hughes trial myself. And right now it needs all of my attention."

"But if you lose, won't it affect the election?"

Roarke smiled. "I don't intend to lose it. And in any case, I won't regret my decision."

C.J. thought for a minute and then frowned. "And you figured Kevin would do fine against a lightweight like me? I'm not sure I like that."

He met her eyes steadily. "I haven't thought of you as a lightweight since that morning you flipped me at the track. I think that your defense of Tony will offer an adequate balance to the weight of the evidence against him."

C.J. tapped her foot, only slightly mollified. "Wasn't it Shakespeare who said something about damning with faint praise?"

Roarke grinned. "Are we back to Shakespeare again? I thought we'd found much more interesting ways to spend our time."

"There's always Parcheesi."

Roarke rolled his eyes. "How about a compromise? A picnic?"

"I guess it would be a shame to waste it."

"Do I get my rose?"

When she held it out to him, he snagged her wrist and pulled her into his arms. For a moment he just held her, reminding himself that he couldn't tell her he loved her, not yet. "I haven't been on a picnic since I was a kid." Finally he drew away. "While you're changing, why don't I take McBride downstairs and persuade the doorman to baby-sit? I think I'd like to have your undivided attention this evening."

C.J. smiled. "I like the way your mind works, Counselor."

WHEN ROARKE RETURNED, he found C.J. had spread the white cloth between two rectangles of sunlight. The moment he saw her his pulse skipped, then began to race. She was wearing only a thin chemise that fell straight from two wispy ribbons of lace on her shoulders. It was the palest shade of blue. With the light shimmering through her hair and over her shoulders, she looked as fragile and delicate as a porcelain figurine. Then she moved, and he felt his blood begin to pound with the knowledge that she was real. He knew exactly what she would taste like and the way her skin would heat when he touched her.

Then his hand was in hers, and she had turned to draw him into the room. His gaze was drawn to her back where the thin silk intruded only from her waist to the tops of her thighs. He had trouble swallowing. "You can't go to a picnic in that."

"No?" When her eyes met his, they held laughter and a challenge. Very slowly, she slipped her finger under one lacy strap and pushed it over her shoulder. "Maybe you could persuade me to take it off. Better still, why don't you take off some of your clothes?" She loosened the knot of his tie, then looped the ends around her wrists. "It's much too formal for a picnic." With a quick tug, she pulled him closer until their lips were almost touching. "Did I mention that I've been thinking about kissing you all day?"

The warmth of her breath on his lips had his own backing up in his lungs. But when he leaned closer, she stepped away, drawing one end of the tie with her.

He cleared his throat. "We're not going out, I take it?"

Her brows lifted as she slipped her hands under his jacket and pushed it down his arms. "There's no place in my plan for damp grass or bugs."

Bemused, he stood still while she unbuttoned his shirt. Each time her fingers slid beneath the material, ribbons of heat fanned out across his skin.

"This plan," Roarke began, then paused, distracted by the play of light in her hair. As he watched, the color shifted from gold to red. Fascinated, he threaded his fingers through it, then settled them at the back of her neck. "This plan," he repeated. "Do I have a role to play?"

"Eventually." The smile she gave him was wicked. "You come in at the end."

When he urged her closer, she stopped him with the barest pressure of her hand on his chest. He felt his heart thud against her palm and watched her eyes dance with delight.

In a quick move, she shoved the shirt down his arms until it hung from his wrists, temporarily trapping them at his sides. The instant surprise she saw on his face sent a thrill of excitement rippling through her. It was so seldom that she caught him off guard.

Encouraged, she trailed her fingers slowly from his waist, up over his ribs. When he sucked in his breath, she felt another wave of pleasure move through her. "Let me tell you about my plan. Before the end, it has a beginning and a middle." She brushed her hands over his nipples until they hardened. "This is only the beginning." Leaning forward, she moistened first one and then the other with her tongue. With her lips, she felt the moan as it vibrated through him.

Roarke drew in a shaky breath. What was she doing to him? He'd felt desire before. Wild and reckless. Warm and needy. But no woman had ever made him feel this weakness, this almost unbearable need. He wanted nothing more than to crush her to him and feel nothing but that thin swatch of silk between them. But his arms felt heavy. He wasn't at all sure he could move them.

She drew back and met his eyes. They were smoky, hot, the mirror image of her own desire. But she wanted more. Ever so lightly she stroked her fingers over his lips. He nipped one with his teeth, and drew it into the moist warmth of his mouth. An arrow of heat shot right down to her toes.

C.J. felt the pull. She had only to close the small distance between them and press her mouth against his to find the whirlwind of pleasure he always brought her. Before she could give in to the temptation, she circled behind him.

"Did I ever mention how much I like your back?" She ran her hands from his shoulders over hard muscles and smooth skin to his waist. "I was attracted to it from that very first day."

With her touch once more clouding his brain, Roarke struggled to remember. "Wasn't I lying on it?"

"No." Spreading her fingers so that her thumbs met at his spine, she moved her hands up to his shoulders again. "You were leading me down an endless hallway. I think you did it on purpose."

When she pressed against him and circled his waist, they both felt the tremor move through him. Before he could recover, she had unfastened his belt, and his slacks were pooled at his feet. There was mischief and a reckless glint in her eyes as she moved in front of him and slipped her fingers beneath the elastic at his waist. "There's something very sexy about a lawyer in his briefs. But you're still overdressed, Counselor." When they fell to his feet, she led him out of them.

"I want you, C.J." He was surprised at the effort it took to form the words.

Knowing that she was playing with fire, she pressed herself against him then and felt his hardness through the thin silk of her chemise. Desire whipped through her, making her giddy.

Roarke reached for her and found his arms still trapped in his shirt. When he swore, struggling to free himself, she linked her hands behind his neck and nipped his lower lip. Swearing again, he grabbed her closer with one hand. "I want you."

Savoring the moment, the sense of power, she stepped back out of reach. "Not yet. But soon." She moved to the table and poured champagne into a glass. "My plan also has a middle. Remember the first time we drank this? I think I wanted you even then." Keeping her eyes locked on his, she sampled the champagne, then lifted the glass to his lips.

With need hammering through him, Roarke swallowed the icy wine, letting it soothe the dryness in his throat. It did nothing to quench the fire that was raging in his center. Through half-closed eyes, he watched her drain the glass, then toss it aside. The small gesture made his head swim.

"Do you remember that night in the hall when you almost kissed me?" she asked, closing the distance between them and pressing her body once more against the hard, waiting length of his. "I want you to kiss me now, Roarke." She linked her arms around his neck and drew him closer. "Whenever you kiss me, I get lost. And when I try to find myself, I find you."

Driven by her own needs now, she pressed her mouth against his and took what she wanted. For a moment she let the heat, the promise, the mindless pleasure stream through her.

While she still could, she drew back until she could see his eyes. "This is the end of my plan. You can make love to me now." She heard the tearing of cloth as he freed himself from his shirt, the rip of silk as he removed the last barrier between them, and then he was pressing her into the floor.

Triumphant, her mouth crushed beneath his, C.J. gloried in the madness. This was what she had wanted. Not patience, but fury. Not tenderness, but savage, consuming hunger. She knew exactly what he was feeling as his hands raced over her, molding, bruising. She felt it, too. It surged through her giving her the strength to pull him over out of the sunshine into shadow. His skin was darker now, its flavor more dangerous. But he allowed her only a sample before she was beneath him again.

With his breath tearing through his lungs, he took his mouth on a quick, relentless journey down her body. He found pleasure, hot and molten at her breast, but he wanted more. There was honey, wild and tempting at her waist. Still he couldn't stop.

Desperate, his mouth moved lower until he found the liquid heat, the unique sweetness he craved. Only then did he linger, allowing her flavor to seep into him until it filled him completely. When she arched against him, gasping his name, he felt himself slip to the edge of reason. Holding on to his control, he tarried until he felt the next shock of pleasure sweep through her.

Then breathless, his lungs burning, he pulled himself up and settled his body over hers. Inches away, he stared into her eyes and saw himself. *I need you.* The words pulsed through him. Had he said them, or had she? Driving himself into her, he surrendered to the madness.

Even as the whirlwind took her, C.J. wrapped herself around him, desperate to draw him closer. Spiraling higher and higher, she met him thrust for thrust until they became one movement. Seconds later, lost in each other, it was with one voice that they cried out words of love.

THE SQUARE IN FRONT of the courthouse teemed with activity. Sunshine and warm temperatures had lured a record crowd downtown for the fair. C.J. shortened McBride's leash and sat down on a curb. A few feet away a child squealed with delight at the antics of a clown. Near the fountain, a small crowd had gathered to watch an artist sketch a quick portrait in pastel-colored chalk. Shading her eyes, C.J. focused her attention on a group of young musicians setting up their equipment on a small stage across the street. Once they started to play, she'd look for Jarvis. Right now she didn't have the strength to move.

For the first time in three hours, the line in front of the Blazing Blue Demons' hot dog stand had disappeared, and blessedly so had the blue-shirted little devils who had been running it. Stuffed with food and soda pop, Roarke's soccer players had run off to try their luck at the games of chance, which filled the nearby streets. C.J. could envy their energy, but she couldn't emulate it. With a sigh she closed her eyes and caught the scent of flowers before it was overpowered by gasoline, tar and scorched hot dogs.

She opened her eyes to find Roarke waving one under her nose. C.J. pushed his hand away, then made a face when he took a bite.

"How can you face one of those after pushing them around on that grill for the past three hours?" she asked.

"Pushing? I was cooking these babies to perfection."

C.J. laughed. "Be honest, Farrell. You spent most of your time saving them from incineration. And the ones you lost you palmed off on the unsuspecting public as Cajun style!"

Roarke grinned. "What can I say? Blackened is big."

McBride settled his head on Roarke's shoulder with an audible sigh.

"Don't you dare feed him." C.J. pulled the dog to her side. "Your Blue Demons gave him more hot dogs than they sold. And speaking of those little devils, when are they due back?"

"Too soon." Roarke glanced at his watch. "I gave them half an hour. Their parents will be picking them up around three."

"What about the dinner crowd?"

"My mother's taking over the booth any minute now. I have other plans for this evening." He leaned forward to give C.J. a quick kiss. At least he'd intended it to be quick. But her response tempted him to linger. When he did draw away, the promise in her eyes made him forget for a moment that they were sitting in a crowded street.

A towheaded boy wearing a blue shirt tugged on his arm. "Mr. Farrell, you gotta see this. Jason hit the bull's-eye, and they won't give him the prize. You gotta throw 'em in jail."

With a sigh Roarke rose to his feet. "I think it's time for me to round up the guys."

As C.J. watched them walk away, she saw the little boy slip his hand into Roarke's, confident that the problem would be solved. He was going to make a wonderful father. The thought caused a tiny bubble of fear to rise in her stomach. They hadn't talked about the future yet.

A deafening blast of sound drew her attention to the stage across the street. She rose to her feet and dusted off the seat of her jeans. She was letting Roarke Farrell distract her again. She drew McBride close to her side and fell into step with the crowd moving toward the stage at the foot of the courthouse steps. At the curb, she waited for the traffic to clear.

Three boys in Monroe High T-shirts gyrated, guitars in hand, to the rhythmic waves of sound that blared out of four large speakers. C.J. headed for the nearest one. If Jarvis had decided to show up, he wouldn't be far from his equipment. Closer to the performers, the crowd grew younger and noisier. She squeezed herself between two teenage girls, ducking low to avoid the lethal-looking weapons looped through their ears.

It was Jarvis's feet she saw first. At least she suspected it might be Jarvis who had wedged his body halfway beneath the raised platform. He seemed to be lying on a bed of wires that cascaded off the side of the stage. Crouching down, she waited for him to wiggle out. When he saw her, his eyes shifted as if looking for a way to escape.

"We have to talk." She could barely hear her own words.

His mouth moved, and he waved a coil of wire at her.

C.J. grabbed it out of his hand. "Over there." She jerked her thumb to the shelter beneath the courthouse steps.

McBride growled, and Jarvis transferred his gaze to the dog. He backed away from the stage.

Wire in hand, C.J. followed him. "I know that you got the bat out of the car that night." She could just hear her own voice. "Your prints are on it."

The boy's eyes met hers. "The police know?"

She nodded.

"I didn't hit Danny."

"Who did?"

He shrugged and looked away.

"That's not good enough, Jarvis. I want to know everything that happened. And so will the police. I already know part of it. Tony had his hands full with Danny, and the other two boys ganged up on Larry. That gave you time to slip away to the car and get the bat. What happened then?"

"That's all I did. I swear. When I got back, Danny was already on the ground. There was blood under his head."

"He was already down? Who hit him?"

"I didn't see. But I knew he wasn't gonna get up. All I could think of was I had to ditch the bat. I handed it to Tony."

"Danny's blood, how did it get on the bat?"

"I don't know."

"What happened after you gave Tony the bat?"

"I heard sirens. I told Tony to run. But he just stood there staring at the body. I took off."

C.J. studied the young man in front of her. He was telling the truth. She would have bet McBride on it. "Why didn't you tell this to the police?"

Jarvis's look was sullen. "You ever been arrested? Brought in for questioning. That's what they call it. If you're smart, you don't volunteer any information. The only thing they asked me about the bat was did I see Tony holding it."

"After they arrested Tony? Why didn't you speak up then?"

Jarvis snorted. "You think they'd have believed me?"

C.J.'s eyes held his steadily until he looked away. As much as she hated to admit it, he had a point. The hell of it was, she wasn't sure she could make a jury believe him even now.

"I didn't mean to hurt Tony. It's just . . . everything happened so fast. He has a clean record. He's a state track champion. I figured he'd get off."

C.J. thought of several things she'd like to say to him, but only two of them mattered. "You know Mr. Farrell?"

"Yeah."

"He's so sure that a jury will convict Tony, he's not even going to try the case himself. So you're going to do two things for Tony. First, you're going to tell him what happened that night. And then you're going to repeat the story for a jury."

"Yeah. All right."

C.J. tossed him the wire she was holding. Then she let McBride clear a path through the crowd.

ROARKE DEPOSITED three more Blue Demons on the cement planter near the hot dog stand. Its position near the curb was making it easy for parents to spot their offspring. He took a quick head count. Six to go.

He scanned the crowd for C.J. and finally spotted her on the street corner near the courthouse. Relief was immediate, but he had to struggle against the urge to go to her. Surely she was safe with McBride at her side. He contented himself with jumping up on the planter and waving until she saw him and waved back. He felt like a fool. He was definitely in love.

Two Blue Demons screamed their goodbyes as they jumped to the ground and raced toward a station wagon. Roarke barely heard them. He was watching as C.J. crossed the street, threading her way through the people who were trying to get closer to the band. What was she feeling? The last thing he wanted to do was risk what they already had. He thought of the trials coming up. If he spoke too soon, he would drive her away.

A piercing whistle made him turn toward the hot dog booth. Gina was there waving him over. He moved quickly to help her unload her van.

As C.J. pushed her way across the street, her mind was racing. A phone. She had to tell Tony, set his mind at rest. Once the burden of guilt was lifted, perhaps he would remember more. A car blasted its horn, and C.J. shortened McBride's leash by looping it around her wrist. Jarvis's sudden change of story was not going to be enough to convince Roarke to drop the charges against Tony. It might not even convince a jury.

Behind her the music suddenly increased in volume. Maybe she shouldn't have given Jarvis back his wire. People were still milling around the fountain, forcing her to the edge of the curb.

Afterward she couldn't recall which happened first, McBride's growl or the push from behind that sent her pitching forward into the street. Even as she struggled to regain her balance, the dog's leash halted her momentum and jerked her back. She felt the burn of leather at her wrist as she fell and an explosion of pain behind her ear. Then nothing.

Far away a voice called her name, once, twice. The urgency in the tone pulled her. She struggled to surface.

"Take it easy," the voice said.

She opened her eyes and tried to focus.

"Don't move." Hands tightened on her shoulders. Something cool and wet pressed against her head where it hurt the most. Gradually she became aware of the throbbing in her wrist and elbow. "This should slow the bleeding," a woman said.

"I'm bleeding?" This time, when C.J. opened her eyes, she recognized Roarke and Gina kneeling beside him.

"You fell," Roarke said.

"No." She moved her head, then winced at the wave of pain.

"The ambulance! The ambulance! It's here." Beyond Roarke and Gina, C.J. saw one of the Blue Demons jumping up and down on the edge of the planter.

When the wail of a siren confirmed his sighting, she gripped Roarke's wrist. "Someone pushed me."

"Who?"

"From behind. I didn't see."

"A big guy," Gina said. "If he hadn't gotten into that blue car, McBride would have had a piece of him."

"McBride. Where . . ."

"Lie still, for Pete's sake! The dog's fine!" As if to prove Roarke's point, McBride squeezed through to C.J. and began to lick her arm. His ministrations were interrupted by paramedics who shooed everyone aside to make room for the stretcher.

Roarke rose and backed away a few paces. He needed a moment to pull himself together, to control the fury that had been building from the moment she'd said someone had pushed her. He glanced down at his hands and saw the blood. Her blood. His fingers curled into fists. Whoever had pushed her would pay.

He watched as the two men from the ambulance checked C.J.'s eyes and bandaged her head. When she laughed at something one of them said, his tension eased a little. He glanced around and spotted Gina talking to a policeman. Another man in uniform was interviewing the two remaining members of his soccer team. Roarke took one step toward them and stopped. The police knew their job. He could get any information they collected later from his connections on the force. First he needed to know about C.J.'s condition. He turned and began to cross-examine one of the paramedics.

When they finally loaded C.J. into the ambulance, Roarke climbed in beside her.

"McBride?" she asked.

"Gina will look after him." He took her hand and linked his fingers with hers. "He can't ride in the ambulance. I can."

"You'll be the envy of the Blue Demons."

"Yeah."

She closed her eyes. Quite suddenly she was exhausted. And then she remembered. "Tony." She tried to sit up.

Roarke eased her back down. "The case will wait."

"No, you don't understand. I . . ." C.J. remembered suddenly that she couldn't tell Roarke about her conversation with Jarvis.

"You're the one who doesn't understand," Roarke said. "You need stitches. And X rays. There may be a concussion."

"I don't need any of that to be able to talk on the phone. Five minutes. That's all I'm asking."

Roarke wanted to shake her. He doubted that he would be able to close his eyes without seeing her fall again, without hearing the sound of her head cracking against the edge of the planter. "Damn the case. I want you to drop it."

C.J. stared at him while his words warred with the pain in her head. "You can't be serious."

"You wouldn't be here if you weren't defending Tony Williams. I want you to back away."

"Forget it, Farrell."

"Fine. We'll strike a deal. You'll plead Tony guilty to third-degree assault. I'll recommend a lenient sentence. He could be out in eighteen months."

C.J. stared at him. "You're crazy! When we get to the hospital, it's your head they'd better x-ray."

"Dammit!" Roarke pounded a frustrated fist on the side of the stretcher. "I love you! I saw you fall. I thought I could protect you, and I can't."

"Protect me?" C.J. struggled up on one elbow. "I don't want—"

"I don't care what you want. Give your client my offer."

C.J. poked a finger into his chest. "You can take your offer and—"

"What's going on in here?" The paramedic climbed into the ambulance and jerked a thumb at Roarke. "Out!"

Roarke paced outside the hospital as they unloaded C.J. and wheeled her into the emergency room. He'd blown it. Now he was going to make it worse by telling Paul the whole story. He walked into the hospital and located a pay phone.

C.J. SHUT HER EYES against the glare of the overhead light. She'd been pushed and pulled, poked and prodded by an endless stream of X-ray technicians and nurses. Not one of them had offered her so much as an aspirin. The pain in her head had been increasing steadily since her shouting match with Roarke.

No. She was not going to think about him. How dare he order her off the case? And if he thought she was going to accept his plea bargain, he was nuts. As for his shouted declaration of love... She felt the panic bubble up and pushed it aside. Tony was the person she had to concentrate on. He was innocent, and he had to be told.

Levering herself up, she swung her legs over the side of the gurney and gauged the distance to the floor.

"Not so fast." C.J. found herself looking into the shrewd but friendly eyes of a small Oriental woman. "I'm Dr. Lee. Ms. Sloan here tells me you need stitches."

C.J. kept a wary eye on the two women as they began to sort through the instruments on a nearby tray. "What I need is some aspirin and a phone."

Dr. Lee lifted C.J.'s wrist. "What happened here?"

"My dog tried to protect me."

The doctor unwrapped the bandage and studied the wound on C.J.'s head. "We're going to have to shave off some of your hair. Not enough to make you bald."

C.J. felt something cold at the side of her head, then the scrape of a razor. "Even in jail they allow you one phone call."

"But this isn't a jail. It's an emergency room."

"It feels more like a black hole."

Dr. Lee laughed and exchanged a look with the nurse. "You have a point. I feel like I've been in here for years. Tell you what. If you'll lie down and let us finish, you can use the cellular phone I have in my pocket."

C.J. smiled at the likeable young doctor. She made no further protest as the two women eased her back down.

"You're going to feel this first needle."

C.J. sucked in a breath and held it.

"You said your dog was protecting you? From what? Was someone using your head for batting practice?"

"No." C.J. began to recite the story she'd already told several times. "Someone pushed me off a curb, and when my dog took off after them, his leash got wrapped . . . What made you ask me that? About being used for batting practice?"

"My usual bedside banter. This is a city hospital. We see a lot of abused women and kids. Not that you fit the profile. They make very good patients. Do everything they're told. I've never had to bribe one of them with my cellular phone."

"Can you tell from just looking at my head or from the X rays what caused the injury?"

"Not specifically. In your case, I'd have to guess the classic blunt instrument. There." Dr. Lee pulled off her gloves. "We're done except for the tetanus shot."

"What about my phone call?"

"Right after the shot."

ROARKE ROSE the moment Lieutenant Mendoza walked through the doors of the emergency room.

"I understand one of our anonymous friends finally got physical. How is she?" Mendoza asked.

"They're checking for a concussion. She needs stitches."

Mendoza glanced around the waiting room. He whistled softly when he spotted the thin, wiry man pacing in front of the nurses' station. "I take it you've finally filled in O'Shaughnessy."

"Yeah."

"How's he taking it?"

"About as well as I am." Roarke sank back into his chair, keeping his eyes on the hallway that C.J. had been wheeled down. "I want to nail whoever did this. What've you got?"

Lieutenant Mendoza settled himself across from Roarke and flipped open his notebook. "Three witnesses saw the guy who shoved her. Your mother gave the best description. He was big, six feet or more, broad shouldered, dark hair."

"It was one of Danny Jasper's friends. Maybe his brother. Put them in a lineup."

"Not so fast. None of the witnesses saw his face."

"Are you saying you can't make an arrest?"

"I'm saying it might be premature."

"Premature? So help me, I'm not going to sit around and give them a chance to try again."

Mendoza gave Roarke a steady look. "Let me do my job, and then you can do yours." He turned a page in his notebook. "We have a good description of the car and a partial license plate. A dark blue station wagon, not new, some rust on the doors. I called a friend on the campus police. He's checking it out."

"He'd better be quick."

Mendoza nodded, then turned as Gina Farrell burst through the doors.

"How is she? Any word yet?" Gina asked.

"I think she's about to join us," Lieutenant Mendoza said.

Roarke sprang up and headed down the hallway. C.J. was being pushed toward him in a wheelchair. He noted her pale skin and the bandage.

"I'm fine," C.J. said before he could speak.

Roarke switched his gaze to the woman pushing the chair. The tag clipped to her lapel identified her as a doctor. "Any concussion?"

"No. The prognosis is very good, if she follows orders."

"Which are?" Roarke asked.

"None of your business," C.J. said.

"Complete bed rest for the next twenty-four hours," Dr. Lee continued, completely ignoring her patient. "If I can't get a guarantee on that, I'd like to have her admitted to the hospital."

"I'll be glad to guarantee it," Roarke said as he took one of the wheelchair's handles.

"No. I'll take care of it." Paul grabbed the other handle. "She's coming home with me. I don't intend to let her out of my sight until whoever did this to her is rotting in jail."

C.J. tried to get up, but the two men pushed her firmly back into the chair. She glared at them. "McBride did this to me. Why don't you shoot him?"

"She's delirious," Paul said.

"I had the leash wrapped around my wrist. I lost my balance when McBride chased whoever shoved me." C.J. turned her attention to Roarke. "Why did you call him? I thought I could trust you."

"He called me because I'm your father."

"Oh, great! Why don't you announce it on the evening news?"

Paul shot Roarke a dark look over C.J.'s head. "I find it odd that I'm the last person to be informed that my daughter's life is in jeopardy."

"I am not in any danger," C.J. said crossly.

"I'll see to that," Paul assured her. "I can take over the Williams case while you're recuperating. The acting District Attorney here will surely agree to postpone the Hughes trial."

"I won't agree to any such—"

"Shut up, the two of you." This time C.J. made it out of the chair. She turned to Roarke first. "I just spoke to Tony. He will not plead guilty to third-degree assault."

"He offered you a plea bargain?" Paul turned to stare at Roarke.

"He was delirious." C.J. pinned her father with an icy look. "And so are you if you think that you can take my client away. Dr. Lee, thank you for everything."

Dr. Lee frowned. "I don't think you should go home alone."

"She's coming with me," Gina said, taking C.J. by the arm. "I'll see that she rests and—" she glanced at the two men "—I promise you that no one will bother her."

"I'll give you a police escort." Lieutenant Mendoza followed the two women out the door.

10

C.J. OPENED HER EYES to complete darkness except for the digital numbers on the clock near the bed. One thirty-five. Almost six hours since Gina had tucked her in. Very slowly she stretched, tensing her muscles, then relaxing them. She was sore, and her head felt tight where the stitches pulled. But it didn't ache anymore, and she could think. Relief swept through her as she sat up and turned on the light.

Paper. She could think better when she was writing. Pulling on the robe Gina had left for her, she took two steps to the desk. When she found legal pads in the top drawer, she glanced quickly around the room, this time taking in the brown plaid spread and the football pennant on the wall. Roarke's old room? It was no bigger than a cell and so narrow that when she stretched out her arms she could almost touch the walls.

There was a knock and Gina stuck her head around the door. "I saw the light. Are you all right? You could take another pill."

C.J. smiled. "I'm fine. The ones you bribed me into taking did the trick."

"Hot milk then. I was just heating some for myself." At C.J.'s expression, she laughed. "Don't worry. I'm disguising the taste with rum and sugar. You'll never know it came from a cow." She led the way to the kitchen. "If you drink it all, I'll give you your phone messages."

"Did Tony call?"

"No." Gina poured the contents of a saucepan into two mugs and handed one to C.J. "That would be the Williams boy, right?"

C.J. nodded as she sank into a chair at a round butcher-block table. The surface was covered with papers, some wadded into balls. "What are you working on at this hour?"

"Menus for the Greenhouse. My daughter sent me some samples from her restaurant in D.C." Gina wrinkled her nose. "Downstairs I serve tossed salad with Italian dressing. At my new place it will be arugula and radicchio with raspberry vinaigrette. I hope I can get used to being so upscale."

C.J. smiled. "I'm sure you will."

"It's nice to see those worry lines disappear."

"They'll be back."

"It's the Williams case, isn't it? So sad, and such a burden for those young men to carry for the rest of their lives."

For a moment C.J. said nothing while she sipped her drink. "I think I know what really happened that night. The problem is proving it. If only..."

"What?" Gina asked.

"I wish there was some way to get everyone together and let them go over what occurred step-by-step."

"Ah. Like in the books. Let them reenact the crime."

C.J. stared at Gina. "That's not exactly what I had in mind. Although...it might just work...." She sighed. "Except they won't even let me talk to Danny Jasper. There's not much chance I could convince them to bring him to Sutton Street so they could act out the fight."

"Maybe Roarke could help. It sounds like just the thing the acting District Attorney could arrange."

"No. I couldn't ask him to do that."

"Why not?"

"He has the election to think of."

"I bet he'd do it if you asked him."

"I'd be asking him to jeopardize his goal, his career."

Gina studied C.J. for a moment. "You love him."

Hearing the words spoken aloud somehow made it more real, made it something she could no longer avoid. She set her mug on the table. "I promised myself that I would never get involved with a lawyer. It's impossible. Do you know what Roarke did on the way to the hospital? He offered to plea-bargain Tony's case."

"Did you accept?"

"No, but the point is that he can't go around trying to make deals just because he wants to protect me."

"I wouldn't worry about Roarke if I were you. I suspect on some level he knew you wouldn't take him up on his offer."

For a moment C.J. thought it over. "Even if that's true, it doesn't change the fact that we'll always be at cross-purposes. We were reading Shakespeare the other night. *Othello*. We argued over whether Iago could be charged with murder."

"Love isn't always easy," Gina said.

"And love stories don't always have a happy ending. *Othello* is a good example. He ended up smothering his wife with a pillow and committing suicide."

Gina grinned. "It's difficult to picture Roarke smothering you. You'd put up too much of a fight."

"That's my point. We're always going to be fighting."

"And you're afraid that Roarke's going to get hurt, so you want to protect him?"

"No." C.J. frowned. "He's always trying to protect me."

Gina raised her brows. "If you say so. Why don't you finish your drink while I find those messages?" She pushed papers aside until she located a small notepad. "Your father called to check on how you were doing three times. No message. And Lieutenant Mendoza phoned twice. The first time was to tell you that he found the license plate number in your desk at the apartment and it matched the three numbers one of the witnesses saw. The second time was to tell you that the plate number belongs to a blue station wagon registered to Peter Jasper. The lab is checking the prints he lifted out of the car."

C.J. set her mug on the table. "All right!"

"Good news?"

"It might give me the leverage I need to persuade everyone to reenact the crime on Sutton Street."

"You can talk it over with the lieutenant. He's stopping by to see you at noon." Gina rose and drew C.J. down the hall to her bedroom. "Of course, it wouldn't be the worst thing in the world if you had to ask Roarke for his cooperation. Men feel useful if you give them something to do, and it helps to keep them from worrying too much or from interfering."

C.J. allowed Gina to tuck her once more into Roarke's bed. It was only then that she realized that there had been no message from Roarke.

ROARKE STEPPED OVER the stacks of files on the floor of his office and sank into his chair. The Sandra Hughes file lay open on his desk exactly as he had left it an hour earlier when he'd gone home for a quick shower. He'd been working on the case ever since he'd left the emergency room two days before.

In the beginning it had been the only thing that had prevented him from going to Gina's and demanding to see C.J. That would have been a mistake. He was sure of it. Sighing, he pressed his fingers against his eyes. He couldn't remember ever feeling this helpless before.

Roarke rose and walked to the window. The muted sound of horns drifted up from the street below. Two days had passed since the accident. Two days, and he hadn't figured out what to do. If C.J. walked through the door of his office right now, he had no idea what he would say to her.

Swearing under his breath, he turned back to his desk and picked up the Hughes file.

"How's my daughter?"

Roarke glanced up to find Paul navigating his way through the room. "Gina says she's fine except for a black eye."

Paul frowned. "You haven't seen her? I stayed away because I was sure you had everything under control."

Control? Roarke almost laughed aloud.

"What about the person who assaulted her? I hope you're going to tell me he's behind bars." Paul perched on the arm of a chair, then rose and took a few steps only to find his path blocked by a row of files. "This place is a mess!"

"Mendoza is a good man. He's keeping an eye on her."

Paul looked at him sharply. "He's reporting to you, I take it?"

Roarke shook his head. "No, but I'm sure he would if he thought C.J. was in any danger."

"You know who pushed her, don't you?"

"I have a theory."

"And you're not going to do anything?"

"I'm keeping out of it, and so are you. Unless, of course, you want to drive C.J. back to Chicago."

Paul sat on the arm of a chair. "Do you have any idea what her grandfather could give her?"

"He must have offered you something similar when you married C.J.'s mother. Why didn't you take it?"

"Not my style. I wanted to make it on my own."

"We were together in your kitchen when C.J. used almost those exact words to explain why she wasn't using your last name."

Paul raised his hands and then dropped them. "I love her. I just wish there was something I could do."

"Yeah. I know how you feel."

Paul studied Roarke for a moment, then gave him a brief nod. "All right, I'll back off." He rose and started for the door.

"We should talk about the Sandra Hughes case."

Paul turned and gave Roarke a bland smile. "No comment."

"I drove out to Farberville early yesterday morning. The young officer on duty let me see the original file on the Alex Day murder." When Paul still said nothing, Roarke continued. "I came across a statement by a Clara Simpson. There was no copy of it in the file that was sent to my office."

Paul nodded. "C.J. said you'd never seen it."

"I'll assume that you've talked to Mrs. Simpson. What I want to know is whether you've had any luck tracking down the partial license plate number she gave the Farberville police?"

"She saw the license plate?" Paul shut the door of the office and crossed back to Roarke's desk. "Let's talk."

C.J. PAUSED outside the door to Roarke's office. Nerves knotted in her stomach much the same way they had the first time she'd followed him to this room. Silly. She'd had all day Sunday to prepare her strategy. She knocked and opened the door.

The moment she saw them huddled together, her hands balled into fists. But anger lost out to amusement when she saw the guilty expressions on their faces. "Plotting against me again?"

Paul recovered first. "That's some shiner you've got."

C.J. waved a hand. "It's from the needle they used for the anesthetic. Dr. Lee says it will fade in a few days." She paused as Paul reached her to give him a reassuring hug.

"You're sure you're all right?"

"I just came from the hospital. I have a clean bill of health." She turned for the first time to meet Roarke's eyes. "I'm here to ask a favor of the acting District Attorney."

Paul glanced from one to the other. "I'll leave you alone then." He patted C.J.'s arm and made a hurried exit.

C.J.'s eyes remained on Roarke. His eyes revealed nothing of what he was thinking or feeling. "My father is usually not that easy to get rid of."

"He's worried about you, and he's trying not to interfere." Roarke sat down and gestured toward the chair Paul had vacated.

C.J. noted that she didn't have to shift any files this time. Otherwise, everything about the room was much the same as it had been on the day they'd first talked about Tony's case. The room might be the same, but everything else had changed, she thought as her eyes met Roarke's once more.

Roarke thought of all the things he needed to say to her. "I want to apologize for what I said in the ambulance."

"Apologize?"

He spread his hands on the desk. "I was upset. Otherwise, I would never have insulted you that way. I was way out of line. I've known all along that you believe Tony is innocent, that you would never accept an offer to plea-bargain his case. I was wondering if you could manage to forget the whole incident?'

"The plea bargain?" C.J. asked, but she was remembering his shouted declaration of love.

"And anything else I might have said that I shouldn't have."

She felt her stomach plummet as she carefully folded her hands in her lap. "Of course. Consider it forgotten."

For a moment Roarke hesitated. Then he managed a smile and said, "You have a favor to ask?"

"Yes." She forced herself to concentrate on the purpose of her visit. "I'd like you to come up to Sutton Street at one o'clock this afternoon. I've invited everyone involved in Tony's case to meet me there."

"You what? How in the . . . ?" He was almost shouting. He rose abruptly and walked to the window, trying to control the urge to go to her. To throttle her? To kiss her? When he turned back to her, he had regained control. "You agreed not to press charges, didn't you? So it must have been the brother? Peter? He pushed you and wrote the notes?"

She nodded.

"Do you know why?"

"Anger. Maybe some guilt. He wanted to make sure Tony was punished, and he found out I worked in Paul's office. Some of my father's reputation rubbed off on me in spite of all my efforts. He was afraid I might get Tony off, so he wanted to scare me."

"What do you plan to do up on Sutton Street?"

"We're going to reenact everything that happened."

"My God, C.J., do you know what kind of risk you're taking?" He walked back to the desk. "Why can't you leave it to the courts? What can you hope to get out of this?"

"The truth. I think everyone needs to face what really happened that night. And I'm not sure that the answer will be found in a courtroom."

Roarke drew in a breath and let it out. He was handling it all wrong. Hadn't he just told Paul to back off? He returned to his chair. "How do you plan to get at the truth?"

"I'm going to improvise."

Roarke stared at her. Would she never cease to surprise him? "Why do you want me to be there?"

"Kevin Wilson isn't happy with my plan."

"So you're asking me to handle Kevin." He leaned forward. "I have a better idea. Things could get violent if you reenact the fight. I'll stand in for Danny Jasper."

"Lieutenant Mendoza is assigning one of his men to do that."

"I've studied those statements as often as you have. I got the indictment. You couldn't get a better man for the job."

Or a worse one, C.J. thought. "You're asking me to trust you with my client's life."

"Yeah."

And for better or worse, she did. "I'll see you at one."

It was only as she shut the door of his office that Roarke could relax.

FOUR HOURS LATER, C.J. ignored the trickle of sweat running down her back while she studied the tableau the boys had formed at the mouth of the Sutton Street alley. The rising temperature had driven Mr. and Mrs. Jasper along with Kevin Wilson to seek relief in the narrow strip of shade along the campus side of the street. Lieutenant Mendoza had stationed men at either end of the block to reroute traffic.

C.J. glanced down at the sketches on her clipboard, then backed up a few steps to view the scene from a different angle.

Roarke was sitting next to Danny on the curb near the spot where Danny had fallen that night. Beyond them, the other young men had taken various positions in the alley. It was the second time that they had tried to reconstruct the fight and the events leading up to it. Both times Roarke had kept Danny close to his side, following his directions or occasionally letting the others tell him what to do or say.

From what C.J. could observe, Danny seemed to be holding up pretty well. His memory of the walk down the street was at least as good as Tony's. That had to be a good sign. And his movements were well coordinated. The only time that his injury became obvious was when he spoke. His speech was clear, but slow. The blow had severely affected his language center.

C.J. glanced down at her clipboard again. "It's not right yet. Look around and see if anyone is out of place." The first attempt at reconstructing the fight had taken almost an hour, but the second time things had gone much more smoothly. Thanks in large part to Roarke, the initial tension between the boys had been replaced by a tentative comradery as they worked to recall forgotten details. He had the same kind of rapport with the young men that he had with his Blazing Blue Demons.

She stepped up on the curb past Roarke and Danny.

"Larry, on the map in my office, you placed your dot closer to Danny." When Larry moved obediently into position, C.J. shook her head. "No, go back and try to remember how you got closer on the night of the fight."

"I remember shoving Bruce. I came in low." He demonstrated, pushing the boy farther up the alley. "Then I turned—"

"I was ready for him," Peter Jasper said. As he spoke, the two boys moved toward each other, like dancers performing slow-motion choreography. "I hit him in the stomach." Larry staggered back a few steps.

Peter frowned. "No, you went farther than that. I hit you hard." Following directions, Larry moved off the curb beyond where Roarke and Danny were seated.

"Is that right, Larry?" C.J. asked.

"No, I was up on the sidewalk when I heard someone scream." He stepped around Roarke. "I remember I had to turn around to see what had happened...."

"What exactly did you see?" C.J. asked.

"Danny on the ground. And Tony... I was closer to him, close enough to touch him." Larry placed his hand on Tony's arm. "I remember I told him to run."

"I still say I hit him hard enough to send him into the street," Peter said.

"We'll see what happens the next time through." C.J. waved the boys closer, then waited while Roarke gave Danny a hand and pulled him easily to his feet. "This time we'll do it without interruptions. And I want you to really get into it."

"You want us to really fight?" Peter asked.

"No punches, but pushing and shoving is allowed. So, Danny, you'll stay with me and watch. Mr. Farrell will take your place alone this time. The rest of you, try to remember exactly what you were thinking and feeling that night. That's what actors do to make their performances more real. The more energy you put into the movements, the more real the feelings should get."

"You want me to get the bat this time?" Jarvis asked.

C.J. met several startled glances, including Roarke's. "Jarvis has admitted that he went for the bat the night of the fight. We're going to substitute a plastic one. It's in the trunk of Lieutenant Mendoza's car. Any other questions?"

"Yeah. How many times do we have to go through this?" Peter Jasper asked.

"This could be the last time if you do what I'm asking and really think back to what you were feeling that night."

For a moment no one moved. Then Jarvis turned and started for the corner. "Hey, it's hot out. Let's do it, and get it right this time." Roarke was the first to follow Jarvis, and the others quickly fell in step behind him.

C.J. barely had time to let out the breath she was holding when Lieutenant Mendoza joined her. "How much longer, do you think?" He flicked a glance at Danny. "Jasper Senior is making noises."

"I'll talk . . . to him," Danny said.

"Nice boy," C.J. said, shading her eyes as she watched him join his father on the steps of the physics building. Mrs. Jasper stood near Mrs. Rinaldi and Mrs. Williams.

"Yeah. He's concerned about his brother." Mendoza shoved his hands into his pockets and rocked back on his heels. "Jasper isn't the only one complaining. The merchants are getting antsy, too. I told them two hours for the barricades. 'Course, you got the acting District Attorney on your side."

C.J. stared at Mendoza as he walked back to join the others. He was right. Roarke was on her side. She hadn't questioned that once all afternoon. As she hurried down the street to the corner, Danny caught up with her. "Thanks," she said.

"My . . . father worries."

C.J. grinned. "Mine, too. I had to bribe his secretary to keep him away from here today. Otherwise he'd be poking his nose in, offering advice . . ." Her voice trailed off as the thought struck her that Roarke had done none of those things. He was doing exactly what he said he'd do. No more and no less.

At that moment, Jarvis, Tony and Larry began to make their way in a jagged path across the street. Just as they reached the curb, Peter Jasper led his group around the corner. The high school boys, smaller and leaner, marched three abreast in front of the college students. Their voices were louder this time as the first barbed comments were exchanged.

Jarvis made the first move, pivoting to poke Peter in the shoulder. He was rewarded with a shove that sent him staggering into the street.

C.J. felt a quick surge of adrenaline and crossed her fingers behind her back. Timing would be everything. Right on cue, Roarke jammed Tony into a wall. Bruce and Larry faced off, and Jarvis sprinted to the mouth of the alley only to be grabbed and spun around by Peter.

It seemed to C.J. that everything began to happen at once. She moved quickly up the street with Danny by her side as the boys splintered into mismatched couples, their movements mimicking the jerky rhythms of a modern-jazz dance. Bodies came together and then flew apart. Only the blows were fake. The ragged breathing and grunts sounded all too real.

Out of the corner of her eye, C.J. saw Tony pin Roarke to the hood of a car just as Larry and Bruce began to circle each other up on the sidewalk. Jarvis broke away from Peter and raced for the car at the same moment that Bruce staggered back up the alley, and Roarke delivered an uppercut that sent Tony sprawling into the street.

For a moment, it seemed to C.J. that no one moved. Then Danny's grip on her arm tightened as Tony struggled to his feet. Roarke walked toward him. Neither could see Peter barrel into Larry, sending him on a collision course.

Just as Roarke pulled back his arm to hit Tony, Larry slammed into his side spinning him part way around and toppling him over. He fell heavily, and C.J. had a clear view of his head when it connected with the curb.

She felt the fear bubble up and lodge in her throat. Only Danny's hand on her arm kept her from running to Roarke. For a moment, Tony crouched low over the body blocking her view. When he rose, Jarvis handed him the bat.

At her side, Mendoza said, "That's how the blood got on the bat. He got it on his hands when he touched the body."

"It was my fault wasn't it?" All eyes shifted to Peter. "I shoved Larry into him." His glance shifted from Roarke's prone form to his brother. "It was my fault."

Danny's hold on her arm tightened, then relaxed. "No." He walked to his brother and gripped his shoulders. "Accident."

"Nice job, Parker." C.J. turned to face Mendoza.

"Roarke?" She tried to see around the lieutenant.

"He's talking to Wilson. I'd better see what they want to do next." Lieutenant Mendoza ambled away.

"Ms. Parker." C.J. found her hands grasped warmly in Mrs. Jasper's. "I'm sorry about what Peter did.... I... We . . ." She looked over at her husband who had his arms around his two sons. "We owe you a great deal. Not just for refusing to sign a complaint against Peter. Keith and I have spent all of our time and energy helping Danny to recover. We weren't aware how much Peter was suffering, too."

"How is Danny doing?" C.J. asked.

"He needs a lot of therapy. But his speech is improving, his reading, too. And he's young. The doctors are very hopeful that he can return to school eventually."

"Could Peter help with the therapy?"

Mrs. Jasper's gaze returned to C.J. "You're a very perceptive woman. We'll be taking Danny back to New Jersey for the summer. Perhaps in the fall, Tony and his friends would like to help, too."

C.J. smiled. "Why don't you mention that to Mrs. Williams?" She scanned the crowd quickly. "Or even better, Mrs. Rinaldi. She's right over there talking with Mr. Farrell."

Before C.J. could take two steps, Lieutenant Mendoza and Tony blocked her path. "Time for some paperwork. Farrell says as soon as I can haul the boys down to the station to sign new statements, he'll drop the charges against your client."

Over Mendoza's shoulder, C.J. saw Roarke walking away with Kevin Wilson and the Jaspers. Later, she thought with a sigh.

"I'll never be able to thank you, Ms. Parker," Tony said.

"You can thank yourself first. It took a lot of courage to agree to this little experiment today." Then she smiled and, taking his arm, led him to where his mother was waiting. "And as far as thanking me goes, I need a favor. There's this big race next Sunday, the Ten Kilometer Charity Run. If you run in my place and win, you'll get some good publicity to cancel out the bad. And I'll never be able to thank you enough. I'll explain everything on the way to the station."

11

IT WAS AFTER EIGHT when C.J. walked into her office. After three hours of pushing papers at the police station and an interview on the six o'clock news, the case was officially closed.

She started to sit, then changed her mind and began to pace. She should be exhausted. Instead she felt wired.

With a sigh she walked to the window and stared out at the sky. It was twilight, that precarious time when night and day were suspended in perfect balance. She thought of Roarke and how much she wanted to see him. But if she went to him now, words would be spoken, decisions would be made. Her hands clenched into fists as she watched the dark make subtle gains over the light. Why couldn't things ever stay the same?

She began to pace again. The first step in developing a strategy was to have a goal. She let out a frustrated breath. From the moment she'd met Roarke she'd spent all her time planning what she didn't want.

At the window she stopped. Did she want a future with Roarke? And what did he want? Shouting words of love one minute and telling her to forget them the next. Not bloody likely.

She heard footsteps in the outer office and whirled to face the door.

"Why aren't you out celebrating?" Paul strode into the room, champagne in one hand and glasses in the other. He set them on the desk and sent the cork shooting to the ceiling.

C.J. sighed. "How did you hear about it?"

"On the car radio. I stopped by Gina's to find you, and I caught your interview on the television in the bar. She sent the champagne." He handed her a glass. "It was nice of you to share the kudos with the acting District Attorney."

"He was very cooperative."

"Hmmph. It saved him from a defeat in court."

"It may have saved my client from going to jail."

Paul looked at her speculatively. "Must have been a tough call?"

C.J. met his eyes squarely. "I had to make it on my own."

He handed her a glass of champagne. "That's the way it will always be on the tough ones. Here's to the successful conclusion of your first defense case." He drained his glass. "When Ruth told me you weren't coming into the office, I thought you'd decided to rest in bed another day."

"Don't blame Ruth. I told her not to tell you."

Paul shook his head. "I'm not blaming anyone. What you did today took a lot of guts. I wish I'd been there to see it."

For a moment C.J. studied her father. It wasn't hurt she saw in his eyes, but regret. "I needed to do it by myself."

"And you were afraid I'd interfere." He shoved his hands into his pockets and walked to the window. "You were probably right. Roarke and I had a long talk yesterday. He told me I was driving you away the same way I drove your mother away."

C.J. took a step toward him. "No, you—"

"Wait, let me finish. Perhaps it's time we talked about what happened between your mother and me. At the time, I thought I was doing the right thing. Hell, I actually encouraged her to go back to Chicago."

"Was the marriage really that bad?"

"No. In the beginning it was wonderful. But we were so poor." He ran his hand through his hair and began to pace. "Looking back, I can see that it bothered me that your mother had given up so much by marrying me. Maybe if we hadn't come from such different backgrounds..." He stopped at the desk and picked up the champagne bottle. "She always loved this stuff. Even on our joint incomes we could only afford beer." With a sigh he set the bottle down. "Then you came along, and suddenly all the small problems were magnified. I wanted only the best for you and your mother, and I couldn't give it to you. I discouraged her from associating with some of our clients. I told her it was too dangerous, but the truth was I wanted her to stay home with you instead of working. And when she threatened to leave, I decided to be logical. After all, if she went back to her family, she could practice law and still afford to hire a nanny for you. You would have all the advantages that I couldn't afford. It was a persuasive argument. And it worked."

Paul stopped in front of C.J. and took her hands. "Sometimes logic stinks. I don't want to make the same mistake with you that I made with your mother."

C.J. felt the sudden prick of tears behind her eyes and smiled. "You're not going to. I'm not going anywhere."

Paul gathered her close and held her for a long moment. When he drew away, his voice was gruff. "How about some more champagne?"

C.J. linked her arm through his and led him out the door. "How about letting me buy you a beer?"

SHE FOUND ROARKE'S apartment dark except for the light over the stove and silent except for the whirring of the exhaust fan. Nerves jumping, she walked toward the kitchen area.

What had she expected? A fire? One of his special dinners? The bedroom was empty, the door to the bathroom shut. He had to be here. The doorman said he hadn't gone out.

She moved around the counter and turned off the fan. Only then did she notice the blackened pan soaking in the sink. Chopped onions and herbs lay scattered over the surface of a cutting board, but their scent was masked by the lingering odor of scorched food. She tried to summon up an image of Roarke burning one of his culinary creations and failed.

"C.J.?" Only when she turned to face him was he certain she was real and not a mirage that he had summoned up with a wish. His glance moved over her quickly, taking in the slim, straight figure and the neat, tailored suit. Recalling how quickly he could have her out of it, he stopped at the counter. But he wasn't able to prevent the ache that moved through him. How was he going to keep his promise to himself and give her time?

"You're on your way out?"

Roarke glanced at the jacket he was carrying and tossed it on a stool. "Yeah." He shoved his hands into the pockets of his jeans. "Where's McBride?"

"At your mother's. I was on my way there, but I wanted to see you. I . . . there was no time to talk this afternoon."

"Would you like a drink? Wine? Coffee?"

"Wine. I'll get it." She found a bottle in the refrigerator and filled two glasses. "Paul invited me out to celebrate. He wants me to stay. I think in time we'll work things out."

"Congratulations." He raised the glass she handed him.

"He also told me that you've asked the police to reopen their investigation of Alex Day's murder."

"There's some new evidence to indicate that someone else was at the house on the morning of the murder."

"Paul said it was evidence that you dug up."

"It's part of my job."

"All the same, it looks like my father and I have managed to remove two very important cases from your docket. Will it affect your chances in the election?"

Roarke waved the question aside. "I expect to get a new indictment in the Alex Day murder very soon. Thanks to your father's help."

She sipped her wine. They were talking as if they were polite strangers. In a minute they'd be discussing the weather. Why had she come without a goal, without a strategy? She glanced at the chopped vegetables. "How about an omelet? I'm starved."

Taking Roarke's silence for assent, she dragged out a skillet, poured in a dollop of oil and set it over a flame. Desperate. That's what she was, she decided as she tossed everything she found on the board into the pan and stirred the way she'd seen Roarke do so many times. She took another swallow of wine. "Thank you for your help this afternoon."

"Forget it. I'm an officer of the court. I took an oath."

"I don't know of any other officer of the court who would have managed to fall so that his head would land in exactly the right place."

Roarke set his glass on the counter with a sharp little snap. "Look, I did what I had to do. I don't want your thanks."

She glared at him as she walked around the counter. "What do you want?"

"What do I want?" His laugh was short as he took her by the shoulders and gave her a little shake. Then he dropped his hands abruptly to his sides. "I thought I could wait. I can't. I want to know where we're headed. You and me."

C.J. didn't move. She couldn't. Why had she thought she was the only one with fears? She cleared her throat and tried for a smile. "We could always improvise."

"No."

She closed her eyes, stunned at the pain one word could bring, but Roarke continued, "I can handle everything else that way, but not you." He drew in a deep breath. "Marry me, C.J."

C.J. opened her eyes and stared. Marry? Was that the goal she'd been searching for?

The hand that he raised to her cheek trembled. Its pressure was light, but it was enough to bring her forward until their lips met. His were gentle at first, but that changed the moment she slipped her arms around him. Words that she hadn't been able to say, feelings that she hadn't been able to express, she poured them all into the kiss.

His hands made quick work of the buttons on her blouse, then slid beneath to skim over her skin. He could feel it heat and then melt. Hunger raced through him.

Her mouth was as greedy as his, her fingers just as eager as she freed him from his shirt and found the snap of his jeans. With a moan, he grabbed her hands and pulled her with him to the floor. Tangled and breathless, they were still struggling with clothes when the smoke alarm pierced the silence. Roarke drew back, shaking his head to clear it. "What the—"

C.J. saw smoke billowing toward the ceiling. "My omelet!" She scrambled up and raced around the counter to turn off the flame, then doused the pan under running water. She whirled around just in time to see Roarke rip a battery out of the smoke alarm and toss it across the room.

C.J. started to giggle. By the time Roarke reached her, she had collapsed against the sink.

"Now where were we?" Her open blouse reminded him of exactly where they'd been. "Ah, yes," he said as he hoisted her over his shoulder. "I had just proposed."

"Yes." She pounded on his back as another laugh bubbled up. "So romantic. Every time I smell burned onions, I'll remember it."

The breath whooshed out of her when he dropped her onto the bed. Before she could catch it, he had her pinned beneath him. "I don't recall that you gave me an answer."

"Yes," she said on a fresh wave of giggles.

Turning, so that she lay on top of him, he framed her face with his hands. "Yes. Just like that? No conditions?"

Her eyes were filled with laughter as she folded her arms across his chest and looked down at him. "Now that you mention it . . ."

He slipped his hands beneath her blouse and ran them up and then down the smooth skin of her back. "Yes?"

C.J. was finding it difficult to concentrate, or even to recall why she wanted to. "I don't mind rocking with you on the front porch, but I draw the line at learning to play Parcheesi."

"We'll negotiate." Then, with a groan of pleasure, he drew her closer so that his lips were just touching hers and murmured, "Are you ever going to tell me why you're going to marry me?"

"I love you," she said.

The joy that came from simply saying the words was so immediate, so intense, C.J. said them again. "I love you." Whatever fears she had of sharing a future with Roarke disappeared as she leaned forward to kiss him.

When they drew apart this time, Roarke's eyes were serious. "It won't be easy, Charlie."

"No." She brushed her lips against his. "It won't be easy for either one of us." She drew back then to meet his eyes. "Especially if you insist on calling me Charlie. But at least you won't end up smothering me with a pillow."

Roarke's brows lifted. "I won't?"

"Shakespeare scholar that you are, you no doubt recall that that's the way Othello offed Desdemona. But Gina says I'd put up too much of a fight."

"And I suppose I should be grateful for that?"

C.J. poked a finger into his chest. "Definitely. Now about Parcheesi, I—"

Roarke silenced her with a kiss.

When she could breathe again, C.J. said, "You said we could negotiate."

"We are, Counselor."

"I suppose you plan on driving a hard bargain?"

"What are colleagues for?"

HARLEQUIN®

Temptation

Lost Loves

RIGHT MAN...WRONG TIME

Remember that one man who turned your world upside down. Who made you experience all the ecstatic highs of passion and lows of loss and regret. What if you met him again?

You dared to lose your heart once and had it broken. Dare you love again?

JoAnn Ross, Glenda Sanders, Rita Clay Estrada, Gina Wilkins and Carin Rafferty. Find their stories in Lost Loves, Temptation's newest miniseries, running May to September 1994.

In GOLD AND GLITTER, #501 by Gina Wilkins, Michael Spencer, a down-on-his-luck cowboy and single father, still dreamed of his ex-wife. She'd left him and their child for her country music career, but whenever her songs played on the radio, he couldn't help but remember.... It was only after he met Libby Carter that he began to wonder if he could ever let go of the past. If he could realize what was gold and what was glitter?

What if...?

Where do you find hot Texas nights, smooth Texas charm and dangerously sexy cowboys?

Crystal Creek reverberates with the exciting rhythm of Texas. Each story features the rugged individuals who live and love in the Lone Star state.

"...Crystal Creek wonderfully evokes the hot days and steamy nights of a small Texas community...impossible to put down until the last page is turned."
—*Romantic Times*

"...a series that should hook any romance reader. Outstanding."
—*Rendezvous*

"Altogether, it couldn't be better."   —*Rendezvous*

Don't miss the next book in this exciting series:
LET'S TURN BACK THE YEARS by BARBARA KAYE

Available in August wherever Harlequin books are sold.

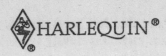

WEDDING SONG
Vicki Lewis Thompson

Kerry Muldoon has encountered more than her share of happy brides and grooms. She and her band—the Honeymooners—play at all the wedding receptions held in romantic Eternity, Massachusetts!

Kerry longs to walk down the aisle one day— with sexy recording executive Judd Roarke. But Kerry's dreams of singing stardom threaten to tear apart the fragile fabric of their union....

WEDDING SONG, available in August from Temptation, is the third book in Harlequin's new cross-line series, **WEDDINGS, INC.** Be sure to look for the fourth book, **THE WEDDING GAMBLE,** by Muriel Jensen (Harlequin American Romance #549), coming in September.

HARLEQUIN® _Temptation_®
IS TEN!

Join the festivities as Harlequin celebrates
Temptation's tenth anniversary in 1994!

Look for tempting treats from your favorite
Temptation authors all year long. The celebration
begins with Passion's Quest—four exciting sensual
stories featuring the most elemental passions....

The temptation continues with Lost Loves, a sizzling
miniseries about love lost...love found. And watch for
the 500th Temptation in July by bestselling author
Rita Clay Estrada, a seductive story in the vein
of the much-loved tale, THE IVORY KEY.

In May, look for details of an irresistible offer:
three classic Temptation novels by Rita Clay Estrada,
Glenda Sanders and Gina Wilkins in a collector's
hardcover edition—free with proof of purchase!

After ten tempting years, _nobody_ can resist

Temptation®

HARLEQUIN®

Don't miss these Harlequin favorites by some of our most distinguished authors!
And now you can receive a discount by ordering two or more titles!

HT #25525	THE PERFECT HUSBAND by Kristine Rolofson	$2.99 ☐
HT #25554	LOVERS' SECRETS by Glenda Sanders	$2.99 ☐
HP #11577	THE STONE PRINCESS by Robyn Donald	$2.99 ☐
HP #11554	SECRET ADMIRER by Susan Napier	$2.99 ☐
HR #03277	THE LADY AND THE TOMCAT by Bethany Campbell	$2.99 ☐
HR #03283	FOREIGN AFFAIR by Eva Rutland	$2.99 ☐
HS #70529	KEEPING CHRISTMAS by Marisa Carroll	$3.39 ☐
HS #70578	THE LAST BUCCANEER by Lynn Erickson	$3.50 ☐
HI #22256	THRICE FAMILIAR by Caroline Burnes	$2.99 ☐
HI #22238	PRESUMED GUILTY by Tess Gerritsen	$2.99 ☐
HAR #16496	OH, YOU BEAUTIFUL DOLL by Judith Arnold	$3.50 ☐
HAR #16510	WED AGAIN by Elda Minger	$3.50 ☐
HH #28719	RACHEL by Lynda Trent	$3.99 ☐
HH #28795	PIECES OF SKY by Marianne Willman	$3.99 ☐

Harlequin Promotional Titles

#97122	LINGERING SHADOWS by Penny Jordan	$5.99 ☐
	(limited quantities available on certain titles)	

	AMOUNT	$
DEDUCT:	**10% DISCOUNT FOR 2+ BOOKS**	$
	POSTAGE & HANDLING	$
	($1.00 for one book, 50¢ for each additional)	
	APPLICABLE TAXES*	$_____
	TOTAL PAYABLE	$_____
	(check or money order—please do not send cash)	

To order, complete this form and send it, along with a check or money order for the total above, payable to Harlequin Books, to: **In the U.S.:** 3010 Walden Avenue, P.O. Box 9047, Buffalo, NY 14269-9047; **In Canada:** P.O. Box 613, Fort Erie, Ontario, L2A 5X3.

Name: _____

Address: _____ City: _____

State/Prov.: _____ Zip/Postal Code: _____

*New York residents remit applicable sales taxes.
 Canadian residents remit applicable GST and provincial taxes..

HBACK-JS